The Author

GABRIELLE ROY was born in St. Boniface, Manitoba, in 1909. Her parents were part of the large Quebec emigration to western Canada in the late nineteenth century. The youngest of eight children, she studied in a convent school for twelve years, then taught school herself, first in isolated Manitoba villages and later in St. Boniface.

In 1937 Roy travelled to Europe to study drama, and during two years spent in London and Paris she began her writing career. The approaching war forced her to return to Canada, and she settled in Montreal.

Roy's first novel, *The Tin Flute*, ushered in a new era of realism in Quebec fiction with its compassionate depiction of a working-class family in Montreal's Saint-Henri district. Her later fiction often turned for its inspiration to the Manitoba of her childhood and her teaching career.

In 1947 Roy married Dr. Marcel Carbotte, and after a few years in France, they settled in Quebec City, which was to remain their home. Roy complemented her fiction with essays, reflective recollections, and three children's books. Her many honours include three Governor General's Awards, France's Prix Fémina, and Quebec's Prix David.

Gabrielle Roy died in Quebec City, Quebec, in 1983.

THE NEW CANADIAN LIBRARY

General Editor: David Staines

ADVISORY BOARD
Alice Munro
W. H. New
Guy Vanderhaeghe

GABRIELLE ROY

Where Nests the Water Hen

Translated by Harry L. Binsse

With an Afterword by Sandra Birdsell

La Petite Poule d'Eau
Original Edition
Copyright © Gabrielle Roy 1950
The following dedication appeared in the original edition:

To Marcel

Where Nests the Water Hen
Translated by Harry L. Binsse
Copyright © Canada 1951, 1961, by Gabrielle Roy
Afterword copyright © 1989 by Sandra Birdsell
New Canadian Library edition 1989

All rights reserved. The use of any part of this publication reproduced,
transmitted in any form or by any means, electronic, mechanical, photocopying, recording, or otherwise, or stored in a retrieval system, without
the prior written consent of the publisher – or, in case of photocopying or
other reprographic copying, a licence from the Canadian Copyright
Licensing Agency – is an infringement of the copyright law.

Canadian Cataloguing in Publication Data
Roy, Gabrielle, 1909-1983
[Petite poule d'eau. English]
Where nests the water hen

(New Canadian library)
Translation of: La petite poule d'eau.
Bibliography: p.
ISBN 0-7710-9854-5

I. Title   II. Title: Petite poule d'eau. English.   III. Series.

PS8535.095P4813 1989   C843'.54   C89-094469-5
PQ3919.R74P4813 1989

*The persons and circumstances of this novel are purely imaginary. Any
resemblance to a real person or to actual circumstances would be simply a
coincidence due to the author's inspiration or to her observations but not
intended by her.*

Typesetting by Trigraph Inc.
Printed and bound in Canada

McClelland & Stewart Inc.
The Canadian Publishers
481 University Avenue
Toronto, Ontario
M5G 2E9

2 3 4 5   00 99 98 97 96

Contents

I

Luzina Takes A Holiday

DEEP WITHIN the Canadian province of Manitoba, remote in its melancholy region of lakes and wild waterfowl, there lies a tiny village barely noticeable amidst its skimpy fir trees. On the map you will find it called Meadow Portage, but it is known to the people who live thereabouts as Portage des Prés. To reach it you must cover a full thirty-two miles of jolty road beyond Rorketon, the terminus of the branch railroad and the nearest town. In all, it contains a chapel, visited three or four times a year by an aged missionary, polyglot and loquacious; a boxlike structure built of new planks and serving as school for the handful of white children in the area; and another building, also of boards but a bit larger, the most important in the settlement, since it houses at once the store, the post office, and the telephone. Somewhat farther away you can see, in a clearing among the birches, two other dwellings which, together with the store-post-office, shelter all Portage des Prés's inhabitants. But I nearly forgot: in front of the largest structure, at the edge of the rough track leading to Rorketon, proudly stands a lone gasoline pump, complete with its large glass globe, ever awaiting the arrival of electricity. Beyond these few things, a wilderness of grass and wind. One of the houses, indeed, possesses a front door, inserted at the level of its second floor, yet since no one has bothered to build for it either a landing or a flight of steps, nothing could better express the idea of utter uselessness. Across the façade of the large building are painted the words BESSETTE'S GENERAL STORE. And that is absolutely all there is at Portage des Prés. It is the image of the final jumping-off place. And yet the Tousignant family lived, some twenty years ago, even beyond this outpost.

To reach their home from Portage des Prés, you had to continue straight on beyond the gas pump, following the same crude road; at first glance you could scarcely make it out, but finally you saw how it ran thanks to two parallel bands of grass which remained a trifle flattened by the passage of the Indians' light buckboards. Only an old resident or a halfbreed guide could find his way along it, for at several points this track divided, and secondary tracks led through the brush to some trapper's cabin two or three miles away and invisible from the main trail.

You had, then, to stick closely to the most direct road. And a few hours later, if you were riding in a buggy – a little sooner if travelling in one of those ancient Fords which still operate in those parts – you should reach the Big Water Hen River.

There you left Ford or buggy behind.

The Tousignants had a canoe to cross the river. Were it on the farther shore, someone would have to swim over to get it. You then continued downstream, wholly wrapped in such silence as is seldom found on earth – or rather, in the rustle of sedges, the beat of wings, in the thousands of tiny, hidden, secret, timid sounds, producing an effect in some way as restful as silence itself. Big prairie chickens, almost too heavy to fly, heaved themselves above the river's brush-covered banks and tumbled back to earth, already tired by their listless efforts.

Clambering out on the opposite shore, you crossed on foot an island half a mile wide, covered with thick, uneven grass, mud holes and, in summer, enormous and famished mosquitoes swarming up by the million from the spongy ground.

You then reached another river. It was the Little Water Hen. The people of the region had had no great trouble in naming its geographical features – always in honour of its senior inhabitant, that small grey fowl which epitomized all its tedium and all its quietness. Apart from the two rivers already mentioned, there was the Water Hen – unqualified – there was Lake Water Hen. Moreover, the area itself was known as the Water Hen Country. And it was endlessly peaceful, there, to watch of an evening the aquatic birds rising up everywhere from among the reeds and circling together in one sector of the heavens which they darkened with their multitude.

When you had crossed the Little Water Hen, you landed on a fair-sized island with few trees. A large flock of sheep were at pasture there, completely free and unfenced; had it not been for them, you would have thought the island uninhabited.

But there was a house built upon it.

Built of unsquared logs, level with the ground, longer than it was wide, its windows set low, it stood upon a very slight elevation on the island's surface, bare to the four winds of heaven.

Here it was that the Tousignants lived.

Of their eight handsome children, shy yet tractable, one alone had journeyed as far as the village of Sainte Rose du Lac to be treated for a very bad earache. This was the nearest French settlement in the area; it was situated even farther away than Rorketon, on the local railway which in some measure linked all this bush to the little town of Dauphin. A few of the other children had from time to time accompanied their father when, two or three times a year, he journeyed to Portage des Prés to get his orders from the owner of the ranch under his management.

It was the mother who travelled the most. Almost every year she of necessity went to Sainte Rose du Lac. If there were the slightest hitch, you could spend days getting there; all the same, since she quit her island approximately but once a year, this long, hard trip, frequently hazardous, always exhausting, had come to be regarded by Luzina Tousignant as her annual holiday. Never did she refer to it far in advance before the children, for they were, you might say, too attached to their mother, very tender, very affectionate, and it was a painful business for them to let her go; they would cling fast to her skirts, begging her not to leave. So it was better not to arouse this grief any sooner than necessary. To her husband alone one fine day she would announce, with an odd look half laughter and half sorrow, "My holiday is not far off." Then she would depart. And in this changeless existence, it was the great, the sole adventure.

II

This year it looked as though Luzina Tousignant could not undertake her usual trip. Her legs were swollen; she could not stand on them for more than an hour at a time, for she was a woman of considerable strength and weight, full of life, always on the go the moment her poor feet seemed a little better. Hippolyte Tousignant did not like to let her leave under such circumstances. And then, too, it was the very worst time of year. Nonetheless, Luzina laughed when she began to talk about her holiday. In midsummer or midwinter, if it were necessary, one could get away from the island, and even without too much trouble. But in spring a woman alone could not possibly run into greater risks, dangers, and misery than on the Portage des Prés trail. Hippolyte long tried to persuade Luzina she should not leave. Compliant under all other circumstances, in this she remained adamant. Of course she had to go to Sainte Rose du Lac! What was more, she must consult a doctor there about the baby's eczema. One of the cream separator's parts had got dented; she would have it fixed. And for business reasons she would stay awhile at Rorketon. She would take advantage of that visit to get some little idea of what people were wearing. "For," Luzina would say, "just because we live in a wild country is no reason we shouldn't be in style every so often." She gave a hundred reasons rather than admit that she took some small pleasure in getting away from the empty horizon of the Little Water Hen.

And, after all, how could Luzina ever have seen a crowd, a real crowd of at least a hundred persons, such as is to be found on Saturday nights along Rorketon's main street; how could she ever have been able to talk to persons other than her husband or her children, who, the moment she opened her mouth, already knew what she was going to say; how could she ever have those rare joys of novelty, of satisfied curiosity, of glimpses of the world, had she not had a wholly different reason for travelling – an eminently serious and pressing reason! She was not a demanding woman; she was quite willing to relish the pleasures of her trip, but only to the extent that they were proper rewards for duty done.

She left toward the end of March. The Little Water Hen was still frozen hard enough to allow crossing it on foot; the Big Water Hen, however, was free of ice at midstream. The boat was drawn over the ice like a sledge until it could be launched in the open water. Luzina was installed on its bottom boards, a bearskin over her knees, warmed bricks at her feet. Hippolyte had rigged a piece of rough canvas above her, somewhat in the shape of a small tent. Thus fully sheltered and showing no sign of fear, Luzina was keenly interested in everything that happened during the crossing. From time to time she thrust her smiling face through the slit in the canvas and remarked contentedly, "I'm as well off as the Queen!"

Two of the children, one pushing and the other pulling, helped their father manoeuvre the boat on the ice, and it was a job that required a lot of care, since no one could tell at exactly what spot the ice would begin to yield.

Without any of them getting too soaked, they reached the river's free-flowing water. Large chunks of ice were floating in the current; they had to paddle hard to avoid them and to make headway against the Big Water Hen's rapid flow. Then the boat was hauled up on the other side – not without trouble, for the footing was far from firm.

The youngest children had remained on the little island, and this was the moment for their final good-byes to their mother. All of them were weeping. Swallowing their tears, and without the least outcry, they understood that it was too late to dissuade their mother from her journey. Their tiny hands, never still even for an instant, fluttered toward Luzina. One of the little girls carried the baby in her arms and made the infant wave continuously. All five of them were huddled together, so that they made one minute spot against the widest and most deserted of the world's horizons. Then was it that Luzina lost a great part of her gaiety; she looked for her handkerchief but could not find it, so encumbered was she with heavy clothing. She sniffled.

"Be good," she urged her children, raising her voice which the wind carried, though not at all in their direction. "Mind what your father tells you."

They tried to talk from one shore to the other, but the conversation made no sense. The children recalled the things they had wanted and begged for the whole year through; despite their grief, these things they remembered very well.

"A blackboard, Mama!" cried one of them.

"A pencil with an eraser, Mama!" another implored.

Luzina was not sure she understood what they were saying but, taking a chance, she promised: "I'll bring you picture postcards."

She knew she made no mistake in promising postcards. Her children were crazy about them, especially those which showed very high buildings, streets jammed with cars, and – wonder of wonders – railway stations. Luzina thoroughly understood their taste.

Her husband lending her a hand, her older boys going ahead to beat a path in the snow, Luzina Tousignant reached the trail, and they all stood waiting for the arrival of the postman who, once a week, if it were at all possible, carried the mail from Portage des Prés to an Indian reservation some fifteen miles farther north on Lake Water Hen.

They were much afraid that they had missed the mailman, or else that he had decided, because of the wretched condition of the road, to postpone his trip a week. Pierre-Emmanuel-Roger and Philippe-Auguste-Emile came very close to hoping for such a mishap; so even did Hippolyte Tousignant, who suggested timidly: "The postman will not dare set out in weather like this. If you were to come back home, Luzina, . . . we'd manage all the same."

"Come now, you know very well that won't do," she replied with a smile of regret, mingled with a hint of mockery, which above all seemed to reproach Hippolyte for his lack of practical good sense.

She looked fixedly up the trail, more determined than ever. After having overcome so many obstacles it would be a fine thing for her to have to return home. A very light snow, mixed with rain, began to fall.

"If only I could go with you," Hippolyte was saying, as he had said on all her previous departures.

And, just as she had the last time, she agreed: "Yes, indeed! To take the trip together, the two of us, what fun that would be! But, poor man, surely someone has to keep an eye on things and be in command while I'm not there."

They said no more.

Far away in the vast, changeless solitude a horse came into view, all in a lather, and on the seat of the sleigh behind it, a great ball of fur, from which emerged a sad yellow moustache, a thick cloud of vapour and, held aloft, a swaying whip.

It was the postman.

He drew near. Now you could distinguish his bushy eyebrows from the brown fur of his winter hat; you could see the gleam of the silver thread which always hung from the postman's nose in cold weather; you could make out his tobacco-stained teeth when he gave his mare a throaty order. Having reached the little Tousignant group without a word of greeting, his frowning glance fixed on Luzina alone, he tightened the reins, stopped, and waited. For this Nick Sluzick was an odd character. In a country where people were often silent for lack of anything new to talk about, he beat everyone for taciturnity. He was said to have managed his business, accepted errands, done favours, fulfilled his postman's duties, made love, and procreated children – and all this without ever having uttered more than a scant dozen sentences.

Luzina was installed alongside this unsociable companion, he moving over a trifle to make a little space for her to sit down. Talkative as she was, Nick Sluzick's amazing uncommunicativeness ever remained her principal – indeed, her sole – trial throughout the journey.

Pierre-Emmanuel-Roger had brought a lantern, which he now lit and slipped under the covers at his mother's feet. He spread a bison skin over her and on top of it a piece of oilcloth to prevent the fur from getting soaked. With all her coverings, Luzina had almost totally disappeared, save for her eyes, which peered out from above a heavy muffler. They were clear, blue eyes, rather large, full of affection and, at that moment, moist with sorrow. All four of them were looking at each other with the same expression of sad stupor, as though these Tousignants, so united in their isolation, were almost unable to conceive of being apart. And suddenly these people, who thought they had long since exhausted every subject of conversation, discovered a wholly new one and began to chatter.

"Do be careful, all of you, about fire," urged Luzina, lowering the scarf which covered her mouth.

"Yes. And you be careful not to freeze on your trip," said Hippolyte.

"Above all, don't starve yourselves," Luzina added. "There's plenty of flour and lard. Just make pancakes if you don't feel much like cooking; and you, Pierre-Emmanuel-Roger, be a help to your father."

The two eldest were not the only Tousignant children to have compound appellations. As though better to people the solitude where she dwelt, Luzina had given to each of her children a litany of names drawn from the pages of history or from the occasional novel that came her way. Among the children who had remained behind were Roberta-Louise-Célestine, Joséphine-Yolande, André-Aimable-Sébastien; the youngest, a fifteen-months-old baby, answered to the name of Juliette-Héloïse.

"You'll be very careful that Juliette-Héloïse doesn't swallow any pins," cried Luzina.

It was the last advice she gave her loved ones. Nick Sluzick couldn't waste any more time. Of all human actions, none seemed to him more useless and unnecessary than saying good-bye. Either you did not go away or you went away; in the latter case, the event itself was explicit enough not to require comment. He spat over the side of the sled. With one hand he twirled his long yellow moustache, with the other he picked up the reins. And they were off through the soft snow, lying uneven on the ground, here in hummocks, there in hollows, which was the road to Portage des Prés.

To describe the difficulties of Luzina Tousignant's journey, seated next to her unsociable muzhik, who only once opened his mouth and then to ask her to stay put on her end of the seat since otherwise the sleigh might upset; to tell how, when she reached Portage des Prés, she had to wait for a week before the next mail left for Rorketon; how she spent those seven days at the store-post-office, which also after a fashion served the settlement as an inn, since in case of need it could afford people who had no other place to go a single room, practically unheated and with little or no furniture; how bored Luzina was while she waited, exasperated at this mischance and greatly fearing that she would get to Rorketon too late; how, when she finally left Portage des Prés, there was a cold wind blowing which grew in violence and froze one of her ears; to recount these few mishaps might be interesting were it not that her trip home was to be otherwise rich in vicissitudes.

III

Once the serious purpose of her trip had been accomplished and her business finished at Sainte Rose du Lac, Luzina's most pressing desire was to get back by train to Rorketon, where she hoped to find promptly some means of returning home. She was made that way; all year long it seemed to her, shut off on her island, that never would she have her fill of seeing Rorketon's brightly illuminated shop windows, the electric lights which burned all night along its main street, the many buggies that thronged there, the plank sidewalks and the people moving about on them – in short, the intense life afforded by this big village with its Chinese restaurant, its Greek-rite Catholic chapel, its Orthodox church, its Roumanian tailor, its cupolas, its whitewashed cottages, its peasants in sheepskins and big rabbit hats – some, immigrants from Sweden; others, from Finland or Iceland; still others, and they were the majority come from Bukovina and Galicia. At Rorketon Luzina gathered the material for the tales she would tell her family for month after month, practically until her next trip.

Yet once she had spent a few days at Rorketon, she had had all she wanted of it. Nothing seemed to her warmer or more human than that lonely grey house which, atop its mound between the willows, looked out upon nothing except the quiet and monotonous Little Water Hen.

She worried about the children. She wondered whether while chopping holes in the ice on the Little Water Hen in order to fish for pike, as was their custom in spring, they might not all have fallen in and perished as they attempted to save each other. She pictured to herself a flood which might cover the whole island and force her husband and her poor children to clamber up upon the roof of the house. Hers was a mind extraordinarily adept at imagining, the moment she was away from home, all the mishaps which could befall her loved ones and to which reality, harsh as it was in that land, lent a certain verisimilitude.

She was on edge.

But the coming of spring had been unusually delayed that year by heavy snowfalls followed by rain and finally by renewed cold. The wretched road between Rorketon and Portage des Prés had become impassable. Even the mailman refused to chance it. Now in those countries of the North, everyone takes it for granted that when the mailman cannot get through, no one can get through. The mail in that awesome wilderness remains the great, the most important business, and only obstacles truly insurmountable can stop it.

Nevertheless Luzina everywhere made inquiries – at the post office, in the stores, at the hotel – to see whether someone might know of a person who was going to try to reach Portage des Prés in spite of everything. At that moment the town was full of travellers, detained in Rorketon precisely because of the bad condition of the roads. And so Luzina made a number of acquaintance-ships; to some few of these she would even send letters later on, giving news of her return and of events at the ranch, so interested in her had these people seemed and so anxious to wish her well. Because of her affability Luzina had made a number of friends during her travels; she still wrote regularly to an old lady who had grown most affectionate toward her during the short train ride from Sainte Rose du Lac to Rorketon ten years earlier, a Madame Lacoste who lived in the province of Quebec. In fact Luzina said that meeting likable people was the real pleasure of travelling. She enjoyed being helpful to those who happened to be at hand, and to such good purpose that rarely did she fail to find in her journeying agreeable people ready to do as much for her. This time, however, no one could help her. She was advised to speak to the postman on the Rorketon-Portage des Prés route, who would deliver her to the place where Nick Sluzick took over the mail.

Now this Rorketon postman was the most baffling fellow of all. Ivan Bratislovski nearly always said he was going to do the opposite of what he did, a kind of peasant's stratagem against fate, which perhaps he thus hoped to best. And probably for the same reason he complained endlessly. At all hours of the day he was to be found in the Chinese restaurant, eager to pick a quarrel with anyone who might have dared deny that he, Ivan Bratislovski, lived a dog's life. Were you only to agree with him on that point, the little Ruthenian could prove himself most useful. Luzina was unaware of this method of appeasement. Having sent a small boy twice to ask the Ruthenian whether he would be leaving the following morning, she had been informed that "Ivan Bratislovski's horse had been injured, that the sleigh was very small to carry a woman travelling with a lot of belongings, and that, in any case, he was on the point of offering his resignation to the postal authorities." What this meant was that Ivan Bratislovski would shortly take his chances and start for Portage des Prés, which, of course, was beyond Luzina's guessing. Meanwhile a Jewish merchant from Dauphin arrived at the hotel where Luzina was staying. He was in a hurry, anxious to get to Portage des Prés with an eye to a deal in muskrat skins that might at any moment be snatched away, right from under his nose. He rented a horse and sleigh. The next morning he left, Luzina with him.

IV

The two travellers had scarcely passed Rorketon's last farmsteads when they found themselves in a lonely expanse, entirely covered with a thin layer of sparkling

ice. The fine-grained, shifting snow was wholly impris-
oned, as though in an envelope of brilliant cellophane. No
breath of wind disturbed this frozen whiteness. Here was
the hard and perfect motionlessness which the cold in its
full virulence demands.

The road was as completely frozen as the fields, as all
the countryside, flat and lifeless. At times it stretched out
like a congealed pond, blue and level; the runners of the
sleigh began to slide to and fro as though they were waltz-
ing; in other places the frost had solidified the hollows and
unevennesses of the road into a surface so rugged that the
vehicle plunged, reared up, crashed down again in a
straining effort strange to behold in a landscape so broad
and unfeeling.

The horse was soon in a lather. The ice shattered
beneath its shoes in long sharp splinters which cruelly
wounded it. Luzina could scarcely bear watching the poor
beast, and despite her desire to get home as soon as possible, she kept urging the Jew to spare the animal.

It took them hours to cover a few miles. The ice grew
smoother and smoother. At one corner they took a little
quickly the sleigh upset, tumbling Luzina, her suitcase,
and all her bundles some feet off the road. Abe Zlutkin
ran to her help. Her heavy clothing had protected her, her
and her most fragile gift, which as she fell she clasped
within her arms. She had not even a scratch. She began to
laugh and, after a thoughtful moment, Abe Zlutkin did
too.

He was a small, swarthy man, active, thin, always wor-
rying and calculating. He had barely left Rorketon at
daybreak when he began regretting that he had taken this
woman with him. She might be injured if they had an
accident; were that to happen, her husband would probably claim damages. Because he had wanted the three dollars Luzina had offered, Abe Zlutkin half foresaw that he
would lose hundreds. He had been shaken by that very
fear when Luzina stumbled back to her feet, more nimble
than ever, and began to laugh. At once optimism replaced

anxiety in Zlutkin's changeable soul. Such a woman, healthy and fearless, could not bring bad luck to him who helped her. On the contrary, he should make the best of it, put himself under her star, which was certainly a fortunate one. A half an hour after the accident Zlutkin was still chuckling over it, filled with amazement and henceforward certain that his good deed would be repaid a hundred fold, in fine furs, in choice skins which he would acquire at small expense in Portage des Prés.

Seeing him so well disposed, Luzina began to chat. She was on her return journey; the horse's every step, however hesitant, brought her nearer home; she was grateful to Abe Zlutkin; she could not prevent her generous nature from offering what she had to give, which amounted to the stories of half-a-hundred adventures in her life that might have been tragic and that always had – she never gave herself any reason why – the happiest possible endings. In the goodness of her heart she really hoped that by means of all her tales she could distract her companion from the dangers continually confronting them both. Yet she feared she might seem selfish if she talked only about her own good fortune. She asked the fur merchant whether he was married. Stout Luzina's motherly kindness, her warm, inquiring eyes, her eager interest in others, her whole nature invited confidence.

Abe Zlutkin took advantage of an interval when the road was a trifle less slippery to show her a photo of his wife. It portrayed a plump young Jewish woman of dark complexion. Abe bethought himself that he loved her dearly. For a moment the business he was in such a hurry to transact ceased tormenting him. Such was Luzina's power. She disposed people to become aware that they had reasons for being happy.

When they were tired of talking, they rested by reflecting on the pleasant things that had been said. Her life, at the only times when she could give it much thought, while she was jolting along on her travels, seemed truly wonderful. Dwelling so far from all the world, she had encountered human beings of all races and characters. The most exciting romance could not have offered her so great a variety of people: little old bearded Poles, Slav postmen, halfbreed guides, Russian Orthodox; once she had even made the trip home with the post office inspector. No one of them had ever treated her disrespectfully; Luzina had only to put herself under a human being's protection for him to behave toward her exactly as she wished. Moreover, travelling in itself had taught her lessons of an unexpected sort: it had shown her that human nature everywhere is excellent. The Jews were about the only folk she had had no opportunity to study; yet, deciding on the basis of her fur merchant that they were rather on the likable side, she let herself drift into a feeling of vague benevolence, lazy and easygoing, which embraced very nearly the whole human race.

But she had to resume the conversation. Zlutkin was becoming uneasy again; the road continued to be just as bad; the horse was limping. And before they had covered much more ground, the sky began to cloud over. Strange red streaks, low on the horizon, foretold a change in the weather. The two travellers were obliged to find a stopping place. It turned out to be one of those solitary farms such as were to be found every three or four miles along the Portage des Prés road. The house was poor; it contained only one room, furnished in back, behind the stove, with a number of beds. Yet the moment Luzina entered their home, shivering with cold, the man and woman of the house came forward to greet her, smiling, their arms extended to relieve her of all her bundles. They led her to the stove and at once offered her food, all this with so much alacrity that she could not harbour the least doubt of the sincerity of their welcome, even though it was expressed in a foreign tongue. It was just as she had always thought: every human being, the moment necessity forces us to seek his kindness, eagerly offers it in our behalf.

After supper Luzina settled herself for an interesting evening.

The family were Icelanders, a people with whom she had not yet had occasion to become acquainted. She noticed that they constantly drank very strong coffee and that, instead of putting sugar in their cups, they placed a lump on their tongues or between their teeth before drinking the burning liquid. When they began talking in their own language, she was even more delighted. Peculiarities, customs, and a language that were foreign to her, rather than putting her off, seemed to give life an inexhaustible attraction.

She did not want to be outdone in amiability by such kindly hosts. So, even though she had no assurance that they understood her, she began giving an account of the road she would have to travel to reach her home on the island in the Little Water Hen. Visiting was what gave them the greatest pleasure, said she. Laughingly she granted that it was the habit of living so far away from people that made her become so talkative whenever she had a chance. When she laughed, through politeness the Icelanders pretended to want to laugh also. Thereupon she dug into her purse, seeking some little keepsake she might offer their children. She had only the crayons and the postcards bought for her own offspring; she hesitated a lot, but reflecting – and with good reason – that her own would not have hesitated to share their crayons with the young Bjorgssons, she beckoned to them, and the crayons were duly distributed. Seemingly the parents were touched, for they arose again to offer everyone coffee.

The next morning the travellers had a slightly less slippery road; the clouds, however, hung low; the sky was mottled. A little snow had fallen during the night. The wind swept strongly through this fresh snow, and there was reason to fear that a real gale was in the offing. They did not reach Portage des Prés until midafternoon, having twice wandered off the track, and they were pierced with cold, famished, their eyes scorched by the wind. The worst of the trip was still ahead of Luzina.

V

That North country, with its vast, sparse forests and its equally vast lakes, that land of water and dwarf trees, has, of all regions, the most capricious climate. From one day to another the ice melted on the trail between Portage des Prés and the Tousignant ranch; you could almost see the snow disappear. Another cold wave had been expected, but during the night Luzina spent at the settlement store a south wind had blown up. Almost warm, soft and damp, a wind swollen with hope – at any other time it would have rejoiced Luzina's heart. With this wind returned the fast grey teal, the green-necked mallard, the wild goose and its plaintive cry, the gallant little silver-bellied water hens, many sorts of duck, bustling and winsome, the whole great aquatic tribe, exquisite companion of spring and of man's assurance throughout these faraway realms.

In less than twenty-four hours, however, the whole countryside had turned into a kind of perilous marsh, deep and treacherous. Under the flaccid snow a man's foot found water everywhere, everywhere seeping water.

All the same, Luzina decided to leave. Either she would succeed in reaching home that very day, or else she would have to wait idly for weeks until the road dried out. For her children she still had some postcards and, herself childlike, she could not wait to give them their present, so that she might watch their guileless eyes brighten with joy. For Hippolyte she had a handsome necktie, which he would have a chance to wear on his next trip, within a few months. She was itching with desire to tell about how the Bjorgssons had received her. Above all she had with her, this year like the other years, the gift of gifts, so precious that Luzina dared not entrust it to anyone and kept it scrupulously wrapped. This gift was supposed to be a great surprise for her family who, truth to tell, rather expected it, since Luzina, ever generous, would surely come home this time with as much as she had always brought before.

Her happiness, no more than the wind of springtime, the warm wind, alive and friendly, could wait to spread abroad.

Hippolyte would scold her for having taken to the road on so bad a day. So much the worse! Today you could still chance the trip; tomorrow opportunity might be lacking, or the trail might be even worse. She gathered her things together and through the store window began to watch for the moment when Nick Sluzick, lately arrived, would be ready to depart. As a matter of fact, she had not saved any time by journeying with Abe Zlutkin rather than with Ivan Bratislovski because, whatever happened, Nick Sluzick had to wait for the mail brought by the latter before he could begin to distribute it over his own territory.

At last Luzina saw that the mail bags had been piled up on the back of the sleigh. Immediately, she rushed over to take her place beside a Nick Sluzick more gloomy than ever; without good day or greeting, without comment or question, the ancient Ukrainian cleared his nostrils with his fingers, then briskly gave his mare the whip.

Today he was especially out of humour; he had had all the trouble in the world getting through certain stretches of the road, and he suspected that the return trip would be even more disagreeable. Not that Nick Sluzick feared the water holes for the sake of his own tough hide; it took more than an icy bath to disconcert him. But he did not like to see a woman running such risks. In general he had no fondness for lugging women along with him – women, children, breakable objects, in short anything fragile. In danger he preferred to be alone. When it came down to it, he always preferred to be alone. A man needed to be alone to ponder his own affairs. What was more, if this Water Hen country were to be any more settled, in the end he, Nick Sluzick, would have to seek refuge farther north.

They reached a veritable slough. Bella refused to venture into it. The old man raised his whip; from the tip of his red nose flowed the usual silver thread; to his moustaches clung the remains of the garlic sausage and bread he had devoured standing near the stove in the store, knife in hand, even though the merchant had invited him to share his own meal. Bella seemed to be measuring the water's depth with her bent leg, which she drew back up under her belly. The water came halfway to her body, about half the height of the sleigh, flush with its floorboards. Luzina lifted her most precious package above her head, thinking less of herself than of this irreplaceable gift. They had, however, passed through the deepest of the water. Luzina, her arms laden, quietly sank back into the seat.

Toward the end of the afternoon one of the Tousignant children, posted on the Little Water Hen shore, heard the summons on the bark trumpet whereby it had been agreed that Luzina would indicate her arrival at the bank of the Big Water Hen.

Immediately Hippolyte and Pierre-Emmanuel-Roger launched the boat. At that last moment two more children clambered in; Hippolyte had not the heart to send them back, so eager were they to see their mother again. They rowed quickly; they raced across the little island. From afar they could already see the motionless sleigh and two human figures, one of them peevish, annoyed at the delay, and the other waving, excitedly perched on the seat.

They crossed the Big Water Hen; now they were within hailing distance, and they cried out to each other. And then, a bit thinner, a trifle pale, but laughing with shyness and emotion, her face wrinkled in joy, Luzina stepped out upon the ground. And in her arms, as happened whenever she returned from her business trips, Luzina carried the baby she had gone to Sainte Rose du Lac to bring into the world.

The School On The Little Water Hen

WITHIN a radius of fifty miles around Luzina's home there existed in all but two government schools. The one to the north, lying within the Indian reservation, was open only to children of the Saultais tribe.* The other school was even farther away, at the end of eighteen miles of impossible road. It was at the settlement of Portage des Prés. This settlement was growing; and since its population included twelve children, it had been able to make sure of a schoolmistress and a few books. From time to time, every two or three years, the inspector of schools came there to make his report, provided that a whole sequence of fortunate circumstances allowed him to complete the trip – in June, if it was possible for him, and if it had not rained for at least three weeks, and if his car could negotiate the last dozen miles of trail. Moreover, it was necessary that these twenty-one consecutive days of fine weather required to dry the Portage des Prés road should fall before the inspector's holiday, which began in early July. Even so, he had had to delay his holiday almost every time he had visited the Portage des Prés school. The settlement's advantages, however, did nothing to solve the

---

* One of the formerly nomadic Indian tribes of the prairies which at present, like all the other tribes that have made a treaty with the Canadian government, lives in an isolated area where it enjoys exclusive hunting and fishing rights. The whites are generally forbidden access to reservations.

educational problem on the island in the Little Water Hen.

Once more the ducks had started their long flight south. The wild geese also strung their way over the island, coming from even more secret retreats in the North; never would they nest closer than ten miles from the nearest human habitation; the terns, the water hens, the prairie chickens, the teal, were on the wing. The skies over the land were furrowed with aerial rights of way, almost visible to the eye, with all the traffic in one direction. Soon the Big Water Hen carried little islands of snow; the river also took on a lively mien, as though it were in a hurry to be gone, thanks to the large white bundles it swept along in its course, allowing you to measure the swiftness of its current. Sadly Luzina saw the coming of another torpid winter, again without a schoolteacher and regular lessons. Even the Indian children had a better portion than her own; they had a school, Luzina would say. But here, how could we manage? Then one evening, as he sat rocking in the kitchen, Hippolyte found a solution for the bewildering problem.

Never did Hippolyte rock alone; the moment he had sat down in the rocking chair three or four children came begging to climb aboard. He would plant one on each of his knees, two others on the big chair's arms and, thus laden, spacious and sturdy, the rocker would set forth on a kind of voyage, for not only did it rock all these passengers, it also took them for a ride across the kitchen floor. All the while Hippolyte smoked; it was his hour of relaxation. Navigating at full speed and surrounded with thick smoke, the chair was almost at the door; Hippolyte was meditating, and suddenly he glimpsed the answer. It was easy enough; all you had to do was think of it. Hippolyte briefly interrupted his travels; he took his pipe out of his mouth; the smoke grew thinner. Without undue excitement Hippolyte gave utterance to the profound discovery which was to transform their existence.

"Now about the children, Mother. . . . I've been thinking; we could write the government!"

The moment they had been spoken, these words introduced into the Tousignants' little home a relief so satisfying, so obvious, that they were astounded they had not hit upon it long before. Hippolyte had the pleasure of seeing Luzina's countenance reflective in its turn, absorbed, then gladdened and, at the same moment, congratulating him, Hippolyte, for always knowing where to turn. The government, of course! How had neither of them even thought of it before! All kinds of imposing images, solid and reassuring, summoned the government before Luzina's inner eye.

Its seat was Winnipeg, the most beautiful city, she asserted, that she had ever seen. She had been there on her honeymoon, on the way to the Little Water Hen. The government dwelt in a house built entirely of marble imported from Italy; Luzina had heard it said that its construction had cost several million dollars, and at this juncture she literally believed it. In all the world there could not be a Parliament much better housed than Manitoba's. This Parliament was surmounted by a statue of a man who had wings and came from France. Access to it was by a great stairway, likewise of marble. Almost everything was marble in that Parliament. On each side of the stair two life-sized buffaloes appeared ready to charge. The buffaloes were the emblem of Manitoba: beasts with great heads planted directly in their humps, without any length of neck or all neck-length, according to the point of view, and whose feet still seemed furiously to pound the prairie soil. They had been almost exterminated and now they symbolized the province's daring and belief in progress. It had been by Winnipeg's schools, however, that Luzina had above all been overwhelmed. Big schools several stories high, all windows. The government took care of them. The government which ruled from behind the two buffaloes was among the most advanced in educational matters. It had decreed compulsory schooling before there

were enough schools for all the children or roads for them
to reach what schools there were.

Full of confidence, Luzina tore a sheet of paper from
her pad and wrote to the government. She dreamed of the
bronze buffaloes. No other province in the world could
have such powerful animals for an emblem. Canada itself
had only a beaver. In this dream of Luzina's the buffaloes
charged down from everywhere at once against the ignorance of backward lands. The next day, ice or no ice,
Hippolyte was dispatched to the edge of the trail, across
the two rivers, with the letter to give the postman on the
mainland. He was the same fellow as before, that old
character by the name of Nick Sluzick who, although he
had been threatening for ten years to leave for quieter, less
thickly populated country, had continued to ply between
the province's most remote post office and the region's
uttermost habitations, just at the edge of the everlasting
tundra.

At the same spot six weeks later, Nick Sluzick grum-
blingly drew from one of his mail bags a letter addressed
to the Tousignants. Pierre-Emmanuel-Roger, who had
been sent to reconnoitre each Friday, found it in their
letter box, the hollow of an old tree that had been killed by
the frost. The letter bore no stamp. Instead in the upper
left-hand corner was the provincial crest, a buffalo surmounted by a cross, the whole engraved in relief, black on
white, and most impressive. At once Pierre realized its
importance. He ran all the way from the letter box to the
house, a little more than a mile; he might easily have
taken a ducking in the Little Water Hen, so negligently did
he look to see whether the ice beneath his feet was
sufficiently firm. On the threshold Luzina was waiting for
him, the temperature thirty below zero, her cheeks
aflame.

"It's got the buffalo on it," Pierre informed her.

"The buffalo!"

She caught a glimpse of the vastness of the power to

which she had had recourse. The handsome envelope Pierre coveted flew into tiny bits. "Dear Mrs Tousignant," Luzina began to read. She did not understand much English but enough to grasp the good news. She seemed to gather that first of all the government apologized for having made her await an answer for so long a time. It said that, knowing almost no French, it had had to appeal to its Quebec colleague, Jean-Marie Lafontaine, who worked for Titles and Land and who had helped it translate Luzina's letter.

Surely the government had been put to a lot of trouble through her fault; Luzina blushed a little at what she had done. Moreover, the government explained, Luzina's letter addressed to the *Gouvernement d'Instruction* had taken a long while to reach the offices of the Department of Education and, among all its offices, that of Mr Evans, who was in charge of precisely such requests as those Luzina had made. Hence it was he who was answering Luzina. She examined the signature and saw that it indeed corresponded with the much more legible, typewritten letters appearing below it. All this, however, was merely by way of preliminary, friendly as it might be. Luzina found the essential matter in the second paragraph.

In this second paragraph of its letter, the government made clear to Luzina that she had not been wrong in supposing it very much interested in education. It expressed itself as distressed to learn that in regions like that in which Luzina lived there seemingly were future citizens deprived of schools. All this must be changed as quickly as possible, and all this would be changed, promised the government, for it was certainly by means of education that a nation came into being. Consequently it declared itself ready to dispatch a schoolmistress to the island in the Little Water Hen, starting in May and for a period of four or six months, as the weather and the roads might allow, under two conditions:

First, that there be a small building, or at the very least a room in the house, which would serve as a school.

Second, that the number of students be at least six, all of them having reached the age of school enrolment.

The government explained that it was obliged to be rather severe on this last point; if there were less than six pupils neither too old nor too young, it could only, to its great regret, encourage Luzina to wait until she had more children or until she had neighbours with children. If these conditions were fulfilled, it would send a schoolteacher and it would itself pay out of its own pocket the schoolteacher's salary. As for the Tousignants, it would be up to them to furnish the schoolteacher shelter, board, and hospitality.

Hospitality indeed! Her expression business-like, her eyes shining, Luzina was quite ready to turn everything inside out in order to welcome her schoolmistress, whom she saw almost arrived, popping out from among the rushes, her small suitcase in hand.

She also realized how truly she had been inspired not to cease for a single year bringing future schoolchildren into the world. Had she had any need of encouragement, certainly this last educational regulation regarding the number of pupils would not have served as any brake on Luzina's career!

As things then stood, she could reply to the government that she had five children of school age, that a sixth, Joséphine-Yolande Tousignant, would be six years old during the month of June, and that it seemed to her, Luzina, that the government might overlook so light an infraction of the rules, seeing that Joséphine would be so close to her sixth birthday when classes began. It was her great hope, she wrote, that she would not be required to wait a whole year longer merely through Joséphine's fault. As far as expecting another family near enough at hand, she said that that would occasion a far longer delay than Joséphine's.

II

No sooner had the letter gone than Luzina wanted to see Hippolyte at work building the school. The quicker they fulfilled the government's conditions, the less likely, she thought, that they might be turned down. To her continuing great confidence in the government's power there was added – now that it had become more familiar to her – a certain small portion of mistrust regarding the accomplishment of its promises. "They won't be able to go back on their word if we set about building a school," reasoned Luzina. But according to Hippolyte there was no such great hurry. At least they must wait until the snow disappeared – even until the frost was somewhat out of the ground. "Don't worry, Mother," he promised, "the school will go quickly once I can put my hand to it." Nevertheless, she claimed that she could not sleep peacefully until the framework had been put in place. One never knew; there might be provincial elections, changes in the government. That kind, sympathetic Mr Evans might himself be replaced. Luzina's nature, under the influence of the ambition, of the ups and downs introduced into her hitherto placid heart, knew both worry and exaltation.

The site to be chosen already preoccupied her. At times Luzina wanted the school right close to the house so that during her daily tasks she could overhear the grave, delightful murmur of the children reciting their lessons; then she imagined it a little farther away, a small house alone and quiet, as was perhaps more suitable to a temple of education. The school where she had herself learned her letters had been situated in the open country, half a mile from the nearest farm. It had been the fashion in those days throughout the southern plains to place the school far from dwellings, as though it should remain apart from trivial daily life. Luzina saw herself, a tiny little girl, running breathlessly so she would not be late; two long, deserted miles stretched before her; on her arm jingled the small pail in which she brought her lunch; she could never sit down during the trip because of her starched apron; often she carried a fine red apple in her hands for recess time. Oh! those were the good days! Absorbed in her recollections, Luzina then had the weird notion of placing the school at the northern tip of the island, in a small poplar wood beyond the marsh. Kindly Hippolyte was ready to make many concessions regarding this schoolhouse project which she had been the first to formulate. But with good reason he objected that if they were to send the children so far for their studies, Luzina would have to prepare them a meal to take with them every day, that this would mean a lot of work, and that, moreover, he thought it a bit silly to have the children eat at the other end of the island when they had a table, a stove, crockery, everything they needed, right at home.

Yes, but had not Hippolyte himself, when he was a child, had to go two miles to get to school? Had not his school at home been absolutely isolated, as was almost always the case in the South?

True enough, his own little school had been all by itself on a lonely rise, flanked by its supply of firewood and two small cabins at a slight distance, one marked BOYS and the other GIRLS. Yet what was the reason for this remoteness? It was merely because each family on the prairies fought to have the school at its front door. On this point no one would yield. So it had been necessary, to satisfy everyone, to locate the school as much as possible at the same distance from all the farms. Here, thank God, there was no reason for acting similarly. What was more, Hippolyte feared that the schoolmistress would not have foot-gear suitable for crossing the muskeg.

"If it's a city girl," said Hippolyte, "she is quite capable of arriving here in low patent leather shoes."

The moment it was a matter of sparing the schoolmistress, Luzina moved the school in closer. Moreover, she had not seriously entertained the idea of having it built quite that far away. She had proposed it as a matter of form, for the pleasure of savouring the future under its various, multiple, and changing aspects, which added a lot, Luzina thought, to the joy of planning.

At last the day came when Hippolyte asked, "Now about the school, have you finally decided, Mother? I'm about ready to sink the first posts."

She had not the heart, then, to have it at a distance. At bottom, Hippolyte was right. Quarrels were what put schools at a distance in the South. She went out, a shawl over her shoulders, and indicated a spot a small distance behind the house yet not at all far away, right to the rear of the kitchen.

"There," said Luzina.

It was settled; she could never change her mind again, and it came almost as a relief.

The school took shape quickly, a small square building constructed of round logs like the main dwelling. It lay slightly at an angle, between two white birches, closely linked to the house like some faithful outbuilding and yet having its own door and its two entrance steps. It had been quite a task to locate it between the two frail birches which Luzina absolutely refused to sacrifice and which she wished to have, as much as possible, on either side of its doorway.

It was really coming along nicely. The children were constantly rushing in with reports. "Mama, Father has cut out the space for another window frame. Father says that you need a lot of light in a schoolhouse. That makes three windows, Mama!"

Luzina rushed out to see. Halfway up a ladder, Hippolyte was driving nails. He had a supply of them in his mouth and, when he spoke, he pinched his lips on one side and turned them up on the other. Almost all the children stood at the foot of the ladder; they watched the building progress with all the gravity and interest of city dwellers watching the progress of important public works. Luzina's gay nature, after that attack of doubts and nervousness which, at the outset, all great projects produce, had reasserted itself. Now that the school was under construction, just try telling her that anything could possibly go wrong! One day she began laughing, a fine, open laughter, satisfied with herself: "Well, Father Tousignant, I don't know whether there are many families like us, who have their own school and their own teacher, all to themselves!"

This it was that delighted her above all else: a school just for the Tousignant family, the feeling that they must be in some way specially well regarded by the government. The settlement had been required to wait until it had twelve children before obtaining a teacher. Other small places still had no school. Though little inclined to self-importance, she could not thrust away the notion that the government was on her side. Had it not already forgiven Joséphine's age? It had written that it would be enough to satisfy its regulations were Joséphine to have her sixth birthday during the three months following the beginning of classes. And no sooner had it granted this favour than the government wrote again, this time politely asking Luzina what name she expected to give the new school.

Promoted, as it were, to the posts of president and secretary of her own school board, of which she was sole member, Luzina had a lively feeling for her responsibilities. Oh! she would have to think up a fine school name that would not disappoint the government! Luzina hinted to Hippolyte that he might cudgel his brains a bit, too. First they reviewed the geographical features of the area, considering what help they offered the imagination. A small river surrounded the island on its west and north sides – the Little Water Hen. It flowed into a larger river which completed the island's encirclement and which, naturally, was called the Big Water Hen. The island, because it belonged to a man named Bessette, merchant at Portage des Prés, was therefore known as Bessette's Island. The school, however, could not be named after the island's proprietor since, after all, his only interest was the profit he could extract from it and since he had done nothing to further education in his domain. On the contrary, Hippolyte recalled, if anyone had put spokes in the wheels it was certainly Bessette. Without telling Luzina, Hippolyte had already sounded the merchant out on the subject of the school. Yes, exactly that. And what had been the big moneybags' answer? He had replied that in the end the school would be expensive; that at the beginning the government, in order to seem generous, would pay the teacher's salary out of its own funds, but that later it would surely make the landowners foot the bill; that that would mean more taxes and that he, Bessette, already paid enough taxes as it was; that he was the only man who paid taxes in the whole area, and that he was fed up with it.

What a shame, remarked Hippolyte, that he should pay all the taxes, since the whole countryside belonged to him. "A profiteer!" was Hippolyte's summary of the man. Not only was he not satisfied with having acquired the whole island for next to nothing, by greasing the palm of someone in the government, but now he was against education because ignorance kept the people at his mercy. It would be better if everyone in the region joined in distrusting the merchant Bessette, Hippolyte concluded. Bessette had even let it be understood that he would make obstacles for the projected school, and how did we know if he might not succeed, because he had friends in the government?

Little vindictive on her own account, Luzina espoused Hippolyte's quarrels. "Oh well, if that's the way it is," said she, "you're right a hundred times over; never will we name our school after that man."

All the more so, as Hippolyte pointed out, because the name of the island was not at all Bessette's Island. Long before Bessette and the rest, the French missionaries had passed through the region, and they it was who had given places their right names.

That was true. The island was not really Bessette's Island. The local people referred to it thus because of the need to simplify things and to distinguish it from a group of small islands at the entrance to the lake which were called the Little Islands of the Water Hen. In reality their island was the Big Island of the Water Hen. The French had thus settled the matter at least twenty-five years before – men who came here to evangelize and civilize the Indians and to rescue them from the fur traders' exploitation, not to enrich themselves. Urged on by patriotism and by loyalty to the missionaries, Hippolyte suggested: "Why not call our school the Little Water Hen school, *l'école de la Petite Poule d'Eau*, Luzina!"

She was won over. *La Petite Poule d'Eau* was just right! How could they, once again, have so long remained blind to the evidence! The Little Water Hen! Thus would justice and truth be re-established. Then, too, what name could be better suited to a school situated in the very midst of the water hen country? At the very time of these deliberations, had anyone been paying attention, he would have heard their wings slipping through the damp sedge grasses, their little quarrels, their sharp, wild cry, which no one any longer noticed, so much was it all a part of life there – that plaintive note, yet not without its sad sweetness. He would have seen thousands of grey wings passing through the monotony of water, sky, and sedges.

Luzina had had Bessette send her – she had to patronize him; his was the only store – some letter paper together with a ruled sheet to keep her writing even, and this she used for all her correspondence with the government. On this paper she informed the government of the decision they had reached. What was her disappointment when she received a fresh letter from the government and discovered therein the odd gibberish which was thenceforth to serve as reference and designation between Luzina and the Department of Education in all business dealings: *Water Hen* S.D. *no* 2-678!

There must have been some misunderstanding. Attached like a child to that which had cost her so much effort and, finally, gave her so much delight, Luzina could not be consoled. "That's not the name I chose. They've changed my name," she lamented.

Hippolyte asked for a closer look at the letter. "No, they haven't," he pointed out. "Water Hen – *Poule d'Eau.*"

"But all those numbers, and the s.d.?"

"s.d. must be School District."

The numbers, however, for a long time held no meaning for them. In the end, Hippolyte believed that they must mean the two thousand, six hundred and seventy-eighth school in the province.

Nonetheless, Luzina would never have believed that the words could have lost so much in translation. In English their *poule d'eau* had become wholly unrecognizable. Yet she had received too much from the government not to swallow her disappointment. In her reply to Mr Evans, she studiously applied herself to copy the figures, the abbreviations, and even the underlining of the reference. Then arose the question of the platform.

The school was almost finished. It had three windows, somewhat unequal in size, a door which closed fairly well, a floor of heavy planks, some a little thicker than others, but all exuding the good smell of pine. There was, however, the problem of the platform. Hippolyte came to ask Luzina's advice on this point, which was to embarrass them almost as much as the choice of the building's site.

"Mother, do you think I should build a platform?"

"A platform? Is that necessary?"

Obviously not. As for that, neither the school nor the schoolteacher were absolutely necessary. They had undertaken something in the realm of the not strictly necessary, and thus the problem became delicate. Hippolyte did not know how to make up his mind. The school which he had attended only a few years in all seemed linked in his mind to a platform. A platform was perhaps useful to the relationship between teacher and pupils. As he looked at it, the teacher should dominate the pupils, speak to them from on high, as it were. This must be the way to go about it: place the teacher higher than the students. On the other hand, perhaps platforms were now out of style. First question of all, had there been a platform in the school where

Luzina had gone as a child? No, Luzina recalled, but that was no reason for giving up the idea.

They both sat down at two of the little school desks to reflect. Hippolyte had built these before fashioning the door, during the rains which had lasted three weeks on end; they were of pine, a little rough to the fingers, with cracks that caught the wool of your clothes, but they were of varying heights to fit the pupils' differing statures.

There was a fairly large one for Pierre-Emmanuel-Roger, four others which varied in size, and finally a tiny writing bench for Joséphine. Moreover, Joséphine's little desk had two almost precise replicas stowed away at the back of the schoolroom, amidst piles of wood shavings. All the children had constantly surrounded Hippolyte the moment he had begun building the desks. Seeing them throng around him, Hippolyte had thought it a good idea while he was at it and while the rain continued, to be somewhat forehanded. Thus it was that the school contained, in Hippolyte's words, "two spare writing desks." Hippolyte was truly skilful; with a penknife he had carved out a little hollow, almost perfectly round, in the upper part of each desk, to hold an inkwell; a groove, also, to take pencils and pen holders. The top of each desk was not made of a single plank but of two, one of which, attached to the other with hinges, could be lifted, revealing a large convenient box that would serve for storing books and papers. But all these conveniences did not solve the question of the platform.

The more Luzina thought about it, the more it seemed to her a platform was needed. The platform would be most suitable to the schoolmistress when she was seated; she would be easier to see and to hear. The platform was the thing that would make the school.

Meanwhile the Tousignants learned their teacher's name from a letter she wrote them. She was called Mademoiselle Côté. In a quandary as to the steps she should take to get to the Little Water Hen, Mademoiselle Côté had turned to the Tousignants for help; they seemed to be the only people who knew the complicated road to their retreat. At the Department of Education, the officials had only a hazy notion. All they knew was that school *no* 2-678 should be located on an island bounded by two rivers, some place between Lake Winnipegosis and a whole series of smaller lakes; that there must surely be some sort of communication with the outer world. Was it by means of roads, rivers, or lakes? The Department was under an impression that the whole area was perhaps served by a canoe with an outboard motor, which supplied the needs of the area's Indians, but this transport would be under the jurisdiction of the Department of Indian Affairs.

Surely, thought Luzina, Mademoiselle Côté had not been in contact with Mr Evans who, obliging as he was, would have given her better directions. Poor Mademoiselle Côté must have had to deal with some other person who was not posted on the numerous letters Luzina had exchanged with the government. She was filled with anxiety. Mademoiselle Côté, ill advised, might well wander as far as Winnipegosis and there take the Indian boat which, when it left Lake Winnipegosis, did indeed follow the Big Water Hen and thus passed by their front door. But it was a small, uncovered boat, without shelter in case of rain, always full of none-too-clean Indian women. And those people had lice. Serious storms sometimes swept over lake Winnipegosis. From their little landing on the Big Water Hen, Luzina had often seen the government craft pass; its passengers were soaked, worn out by the bouncing the vessel had given them, and summarily scattered among the bags of flour and boxes of lard which the canoe also transported; such a fashion of travelling had seemed to her very primitive. There was another, much more agreeable way of reaching the Little Water Hen. Luzina set about explaining it, point by point, to her schoolmistress, and she hurried at the task. It would be a close thing now, for Mademoiselle Côté to get the letter in time.

She should take the main-line train to Dauphin. There she would have to change, and it might be that she would have to await the accommodation from Rorketon for a half or perhaps a full day. Luzina explained why. The train on the Rorketon branch line sometimes hauled ties for the railway and often empty milk cans; at other times it left without any load at all. Which is as much as to say that you couldn't know beforehand the hour of its departure. However, if Mademoiselle Côté found it too long waiting at the station, she would be well received at one of Luzina's friends', a Madame Lallemand, formerly from the province of Quebec, who lived in a small white house right next to the hardware store belonging to a man named Harrison at Dauphin. Mademoiselle Côté need not have a moment's hesitation in taking a rest at that lady's house. She should, though, be careful not to remain there too long in case the branch-line train to Rorketon might be loaded quicker than expected. Mademoiselle Côté would spend the night at Rorketon. Luzina gave the address of another acquaintance, a Madame Chartrand, at whose house the teacher would find a clean room at little expense. But, Luzina pointed out, it was absolutely necessary to arrive at Rorketon on a Thursday in order to make connections the next day, a Friday, with the mail from Rorketon to Portage des Prés. Otherwise, Mademoiselle Côté would have to wait a whole week for the departure of the next mail, and that would not be pleasant. On arrival at Rorketon, Mademoiselle Côté would therefore look for the postman. His name was Ivan Bratislovski, and he was to be found at the Rorketon post office or saddlery-relay station. He was easy to recognize by reason of a wildcat hat which he wore almost until mid-June. It was as well that she should be on her guard against Ivan Bratislovski's unscrupulous overcharging of strangers. The price of the trip was two dollars, and she should not give Ivan Bratislovski a cent more, even if he complained that he was in desperate straits, which was not true at all. Apart from this weakness of boosting prices when he had an opportunity, Ivan Bratislovski was not dangerous. He was a man who knew his place. Mademoiselle Côté need have no fear of travelling alone with the small Ruthenian. And so with him she would reach Portage des Prés. There she would change mailmen. After leaving Portage de Prés, she would travel with their own Little Water Hen island postman, a Ukrainian by the name of Nick Sluzick. On occasion he also tried to exact more than the regular price from strangers. People of the region only gave him fifty cents, and it was thought to be enough, since Nick Sluzick had to make the trip whether or not he had a load. Mademoiselle Côté was free to give him a little more if she wished, but not much more. Perhaps Nick Sluzick would say that it took more gasoline for two people. No attention should be paid to this. Two persons required no more gasoline than one alone, and everyone on Little Water Hen island was eager to see the schoolmistress arrive and sent her thanks and welcome in advance.

At last it was finished. Luzina did not think she had forgotten any of the mishaps – any of the snares – which might waylay Mademoiselle Côté, but for all that she was none too proud of her letter.

She naturally liked writing letters. Writing the government had not given her too much trouble. Surely the government was in some degree responsible for the ignorance on the island of the Little Water Hen, since it had waited so many years before giving them a school. Moreover, the fact that the government knew scarcely any French had put her at her ease; it would not take any note of Luzina's mistakes in spelling. The government's replies, typewritten and in English, had not greatly disturbed her. It was the teacher's letter, in a beautiful handwriting absolutely straight and without erasures which, by revealing the perfection a letter might attain both in form and in content, overwhelmed Luzina. Thenceforward she would no longer be altogether happy about writing. But the lot had been cast. Luzina had settled the matter forever the moment she appealed for education. Her fate would now be to write, everlastingly to write, to write until the end of her days.

III

The government's gifts arrived. The big packing case contained a box of white chalk, English readers, and precisely
six blackboard erasers. The wall map of the world had
travelled separately. On thick, strong, glazed paper, affixed
to a wooden cylinder, it weighed about fifteen pounds.
Nick Sluzick had worked like a dog to stow it away in his
old Ford – he had had to slip it into the back of the car at
an angle, between the bags of mail; a goodly part of the
map, however, had remained outside, and it had snagged
all sorts of branches along the narrower stretches of the
trail.

Hanging in the schoolhouse, the world map took up a
whole section of wall. It rolled and unrolled on itself like a
smoothly operating window shade. You had only to pull
the string at the bottom for the south polar lands to
appear; then followed Australia, New Zealand, that part
of the world where, Luzina said, it was night when they
themselves had day. What mysteries! Thereupon Nick
Sluzick lugged out another map, this one of Manitoba and
very detailed. Old Nick had thought that he was delivering
wallpaper, and he wondered how the Tousignants could
use so much paper in so small a house. Were they going to
paper the sheepfold? The schoolmistress was already on
her way. That evening, before they went to bed, the
Tousignants had remarked, "By this time, Mademoiselle
Côté has taken the train."

In the morning Luzina mused out loud, "Now she has
arrived at Dauphin."

Toward the middle of the afternoon she said firmly,
"Unless there were a lot of ties to load, Mademoiselle Côté
must have passed Sainte Rose du Lac, and the train is
travelling backwards."

For some time now, Mademoiselle Côté's room had
awaited her. Here is how Luzina had managed to make
free a room for the teacher's use: pushing and pulling, she
had moved a small bed into her own room; with her own

big bed close against the wall, she had succeeded in making room for this smaller bed as well; another bed had gone its way to the kitchen, where it was well enough concealed behind a length of faded drapery. In such fashion there came into being in the Tousignant house a room which seemed extremely large and rich, an astounding room which contained only one single bed.

Luzina had never done so much even for the Capuchin father who came once a year to hear their confessions and celebrate Mass in the parlour next the kitchen. Of course he had himself feared above everything else that he might give trouble and he had asked to sleep on the sofa in the parlour. Yet Luzina might have been accused of giving herself more pains for the teacher than for the Lord, and she strove to justify herself. "Our old missionary," said she, "is used to a hard life, whereas our schoolmistress is perhaps a girl who until now has never known anything but ease and comfort."

Hippolyte had shaved. Two hours ahead of time he had already put on his party headgear. "I'm sure it's about time to get going."

The postman's hours were most uncertain. Yet never did he get as far as the Big Water Hen before the end of the afternoon, and it was still several hours before the time when the sun would begin to set.

"Yes, go," said Luzina. "You can just see that poor girl sink to her knees in the mud along the edge of the Big Water Hen without her having the least inkling of an idea as to how she might cross it."

She herself went off to give the schoolhouse a final inspection. On this large, almost unpeopled island, the little school had quite naturally become the place where she by choice went to seek solitude and silence.

Nothing was lacking either in the atmosphere or in the physical objects to promote learning. Hippolyte had not forgotten the blackboards; he had used a heavy tarpaper which served in those parts as an insulating material or as covering for roofs, and of which there had remained a roll after their house was completed. Chalk took fairly well on its coarse-grained surface.

Luzina climbed the single step to the platform. It occurred to her to sit down at the teacher's desk in order the better to visualize what was about to take place on their island in the Little Water Hen. Was it because she was sitting on the schoolmistress's own chair, up on the platform? In any case, Luzina's vision was much deeper and broader than usual. She saw progress reach them. Thirteen years ago she had come to this place over a track you could scarcely make out in the wilderness. Little by little the grass had been flattened by the passage of vehicles, and at the end of a few years you had been able to see a sort of road emerge, fairly well marked. Then they had begun to receive the mail once a week. Come, now! The year when the Portage des Prés post office had been opened, that same year the merchant Bessette had bought himself a car! Two years later, Nick Sluzick in his turn was rolling along in summer in an ancient Ford. And now a schoolmistress was on her way to the island in the Little Water Hen. Oh, there was no doubting it at all: civilization, progress, were blowing in this direction like the thawing spring breeze.

No longer could Luzina sit still. She took the baby in her arms and, four other children trailing behind, went to the bank of the Little Water Hen and stood waiting. It was a very hot afternoon for May. There was a slightly damp southwest wind which sang over the great, silent countryside. Luzina at its head, the little group stood erect under the heavens, in that wind out of open spaces which made the baby's hair and blanket flutter.

It was a day the like of which Luzina imagined she had never seen; on both edges of the river and almost to its middle the tall leaves of the rushes stirred; the neighbouring island was also covered with them, and they continued far into the distance, growing thicker and thicker together as they approached the broad waters of Lake Winnipegosis.

At that season the year's fresh sprouts had made little growth; so far they formed only that moist background of greenery which was Luzina's pleasure. But last year's dead reeds still remained standing. They were lank and sparse, with ragged plumes, over the tips of which a bird would sometimes veer in flight. Long stems hung broken at the middle, tangled and collapsing upon the living young tufts. A few leaves remained to them, blades pointed or broken and shrivelled, ready to crumble away. All this dead vegetation was faded, of a soft, pale hue like straw, and, even when the wind was still, without seeming to stir, the dry water grasses emitted a rustling sound, a trifle sad, sterile, continuous. They might have brought to mind autumn's melancholy, had it not been for the sun, which drew from them glints of gold, and the birds of the South, innumerable amidst the high rustling stalks. From all directions Luzina heard the plopping of the divers and the sport of the ducklings, splashing as they clambered out of puddles. You saw very little of them; all by herself a small mother duck occasionally emerged and inspected the surroundings with her brilliant eyes. She uttered a few energetic quacks, then swam away, her tiny tailpiece poked a little into the air, angry at all those people along the shore. These little females were bold ones and put on a bold show. By contrast, on the higher part of the island behind Luzina, the ewes lamented more than was their wont; close to their newborn lambs, their bleating was apprehensive. Of all this, today, Luzina was more than usually aware; perhaps – as it seemed to her – tenderness and anxiety were always one and the same.

She shaded her eyes with one hand. In the distance a small group had just landed on Mosquito Island, and a canoe was moving forward, upside down, above the level of the rushes. Ordinarily the Tousignants were well equipped for crossing the two rivers. A boat was assigned to the ferrying of each and was permanently available. But the Big Water Hen craft was in need of repairs; so only one canoe was available that day, and a carry was necessary.

The boat drew nearer; beneath it Luzina recognized Hippolyte's legs and torso, and behind him two others bearing burdens, who must be Pierre and Philippe-Auguste-Emile. Other children followed; from among them Luzina picked out the figure which must be Mademoiselle Côté.

Immediately her heart began thumping within her and fear overcame Luzina. Her eyes gathered in the children standing around her. What did she know about this Miss Côté? Perhaps she was one of those old maids whose prop is discipline and who know how to achieve it only by smacking tender knuckles with the edge of a ruler. When about nine, Luzina had had such a teacher; she had quickly forgotten her, her nature far preferring happy memories. Yet here she was, come back to life, and associated in Luzina's mind with the multiplication tables – that spiteful schoolmistress with her long pointed stick which was intended in principle to point out the many lovely countries on the map of the world, not to lash trembling knees and fingers.

The approaching group had reached the bushiest portion of the island; Luzina could barely glimpse them. When they emerged, they were close to her, and her eyes feasted upon a slender, sensitive apparition such as no one had ever hoped to behold upon the island in the Little Water Hen. This old maid was neither old nor stern. She was a picture of sprightliness. A tiny straw hat, a real city hat, which she wore cocked over her right eye, thrust its red feather here and there among the reeds that in their turn threatened to catch it and tear it loose. She had to hold onto her hat with one hand, with the other protect her pretty suit from being spattered, and be careful not to step into puddles. Her busy hands were covered with gloves. Tucked under her elbow was a beautiful leather handbag. Her shoes had high heels – which explained why Hippolyte had several times had to rest the canoe and wait for the teacher, since because of those heels she had had to circle the large holes, look for hummocks solid enough to support her, and thus cover almost twice the distance he did. You would have thought she was coming to a post a step from the railroad station, in the very middle of a village, and under the noses of at least a dozen families eagerly watching her arrival. Never would Luzina forget this lovely sight.

The teacher drew nearer, seated now on the bottom of the boat. She pulled her skirt down over her knees, finding it a bit difficult to shelter herself from the splash of the oars which sent drops flying over her leather bag, her suit, her valise, and her small hat. "Do be careful, Hippolyte," Luzina wanted to cry out. She had shifted the chubby baby from her right arm to her left; she pressed it to her sturdy breast and prepared to extend her free hand toward the teacher. She was laughing, for emotion had that effect on Luzina. The more she was affected, the harder she laughed, and then the more she laughed, the less she could control her laughter. All this elegance, this refinement, this gracious atmosphere of life in the South which was today invading her island, all this, constricting Luzina's heart, impelled her to a sort of robust, continuous clucking. At the very river's edge, her feet in the mud, the fat baby making her awkward, she kept heartily shaking Mademoiselle Côté's small gloved hand, and amidst her fits of laughter all she could manage was a series of ingenuous questions: "Mademoiselle Côté? Is it Mademoiselle Côté? So you've arrived, have you, Mademoiselle Côté?" as though there could exist some doubt as to the schoolmistress's identity.

That young lady was far from wanting to laugh. It was a mere two weeks since she had received her brand-new teacher's licence. In a white dress, her hair freshly curled for the occasion, she had been handed the rolled parchment, tied with a wide red ribbon, by an official representative of the Department of Education, who had congratulated her on her fine academic record. No matter how clever Mademoiselle Côté may have been, she never would have believed that Manitoba could be so huge and

so thinly populated. To all intents, she had never left her
big village in the South, along the shores of the Red River,
save to attend the Winnipeg Normal School, though she
had done brilliantly in geography as well as in everything
else that could be learned from textbooks. Jogging today
from postal relay to postal relay, from one broken-down
Ford to another even shakier, had shattered her. For many
hours, now, the poor child had not had the least idea of
where she was. When she had reached the Portage des
Prés settlement, she had espied, a little apart from the five
houses of the hamlet, a small plank building which, if you
were hard put to it, you might take for a school. She had
thought that this was her school and, her heart already
heavy, she had steeled herself to ask the merchant Bessette
for the key. The latter had laughed heartily. This was the
village, he had pointed out to her, and they had had their
teacher long since. Mademoiselle Côté was given to
understand that her assignment was far less important
than that at the settlement. She had continued jolting
onward, this time in company with a small man who was
probably dumb, since he expressed himself only in a variety of grunts. And now she beheld what she had yearned
for with all her heart through so many years of devoted
study, of prizes for excellence, and of magnificent illusions: so this was it, her first school, the bottom step in
what she looked upon as the most meritorious, the most
exalted of careers! But when you came down to it, where
was the school? She hesitated between the four grey cabins
of unsquared logs, the biggest of which, in her native
South, could have served for nothing more than a hay
barn or a small piggery. All around her reigned silence,
water, the shrill chirping of the little silver-bellied hens,
their wings spotted with grey. And Mademoiselle Côté's
heart likewise lamented, lost in the wilderness; it, too,
already sought its refuge. Her glance fell upon the children. Half the small Tousignants had Luzina's light blue
eyes, laughing and tender; the other half, Hippolyte's
brown pupils, slow and sleepy. Yet all these eyes, fastened

upon the schoolmistress, displayed at that instant the same expression of loving anguish. Even the smallest of them, who would not yet be going to school, hesitated between fear and trust. All stood close to the pretty young girl like fawns which a single movement could put to flight but which the least caress could tame.

Mademoiselle Côté suddenly stooped down toward the small, wavering band; putting aside her bag, her suitcase, her hat, she opened her arms to Luzina's children. Joséphine was the first to come, that shy child who, at the mere sight of a stranger, felt compelled to slip away among the rushes; then Charles; then Edmond who, as he moved forward, trembled all over and, finally, little by little, the whole small brood, except Pierre, blushing and deeply embarrassed of a sudden, feeling that all these embraces were unseemly.

The young woman straightened up. And then you saw that she meant business, this Miss Côté, and that her youth would not stand in the way of firmness – quite the contrary. She had picked the school out from among the cabins, and she said in a firm, low voice: "I'm going at once to the schoolhouse to prepare the lessons."

"You must be tired. You could almost take a day's holiday before that," Luzina reluctantly suggested, moved by a feeling of justice.

"Begin with a day's holiday! No, indeed! I must get to work," said Mademoiselle Côté.

She was the first to move, straight toward the school, and already it was she who gave them all the lead.

IV

The class had been in session for about an hour. In her kitchen, Luzina from time to time heard an explosion of small voices; toward nine-thirty a burst of laughter reached her ears, that uncontrollable laughter of children at school, nervous, excited, suddenly extinguished; but most of the time she listened in vain; tiptoeing about, standing in the open doorway, she did not hear a sound.

Luzina was not one of those women who are greatly disturbed by her children's racket. Since her nerves were quiet and her temperament dreamy and inclined to see the rosy side of life, she easily became oblivious to their noise by telling herself stories. Of course these stories included sad episodes, even rather sinister bits of drama, but solely for the pleasure of resolving them at the end and of seeing everything rightly ordered in her heart. Occasionally she imagined misfortunes beyond remedy: Hippolyte suddenly was drowned; she was left a widow with ten children; two of her boys turned out badly and married Indian women; but all this she had devised with an eye only to the relief Luzina always felt when, laying her macabre tales aside, she was able to see how remote they were from reality. All usual sounds, the outcries of the hens and the children, stimulated Luzina in these excursions. This morning, it was the silence that upset her.

What could they be doing in the schoolhouse? What was it that had made them all laugh a moment ago? Above all, what tasks could they possibly be performing amidst such silence?

Toward ten-thirty Luzina needed some wood shavings to raise the heat in her oven, in which she was baking a molasses cake, and quite naturally she went to gather them around the school building, where they had fallen from Hippolyte's plane. Far from her the thought of spying on the teacher. Luzina was fully resolved to respect Mademoiselle Côté's independence. That very morning she felt she had settled for everyone the question of shared authority on Little Water Hen Island. "In school," Luzina had declared, "you will obey your schoolmistress in all things." She would not be one of those women who take their children's part against the teacher, sympathize with them for some minor punishment they have undergone and thus undermine the prestige of authority.

Her back bent, her head drawn between her shoulders,

she was getting ready to sneak by the corner of the school without being seen through the open window when a very specific question stopped her in her tracks. "In what province do we live?" Mademoiselle Côté wanted to know.

What a question! Luzina had the answer on the tip of her tongue. Right next the building there was a stump, exactly under the open window. Luzina let herself sink onto it.

"What is our province called?" repeated Mademoiselle Côté.

None of the children answered.

Luzina began to feel embarrassed. "What a pack of ignorant dunces!" she thought. "You certainly ought to know the answer to that." She shaped it with her own lips, syllable by syllable. She concentrated her will on transmitting the word to the minds of the schoolchildren. "What a shameful business – not even to know where you live."

At last one voice piped up, shy and faltering: "The Water Hen, Mademoiselle."

Luzina recognized the voice – it was Pierre's.

"If that's not a disgrace, a big boy eleven years old!" said she to herself. "I'll fix him when he comes back to the house, he and his Water Hens!"

The teacher continued patiently. "No, Pierre, the Water Hen is the name of this region alone; I'm not even sure it's the right geographical name. I rather think that it's a local name. What I am asking for is the name of the big province in which is included the Water Hen and many other regions. What province is that?"

No inspiration came to the Tousignant pupils' minds.

"It is a very large province," Mademoiselle Côté helped them a little more. "It is almost as large, by itself alone, as all France. It stretches from the United States all the way to Hudson Bay."

"Manitoba!"

Edmond flung out the word; his sharp little voice had taken on the very accent of victory. On the other side of the schoolhouse wall, Luzina was fully as proud; her round pink face grew tender. Edmond, indeed! A little shaver not yet eight! Where did that one learn we live in vast Manitoba? But then he had his nose in everything, that Edmond; he was always rummaging around, busy listening to grown-ups. Luzina broadly absolved him for all his prying.

"Very good," said the teacher approvingly. "This province is in fact Manitoba. But it, with eight other provinces, makes up a very big country, which is called . . . "

"Canada," Pierre suggested, in a humble tone of voice, as though begging pardon.

"Yes, of course. Very good, Pierre. Since we live in Canada, we are? . . . Cana- . . . Canadi- . . . "

"Canadians," Pierre finished the word.

"That's it, quite right," Mademoiselle congratulated them.

Luzina agreed that Pierre had in some part redeemed himself. All the same, to have said we lived in the province of the Water Hen! What a fool child!

"We are Canadians," continued the teacher, "but we are, above all, French Canadians. Long, long ago, more than three hundred years ago, Canada was inhabited only by redskins. The King of France then sent a Frenchman to discover Canada. He was called Jacques Cartier."

The sun warmed Luzina, well sheltered against the wind, her back to the schoolhouse wall. She had crossed her hands. Enchanted, she listened to the lovely, old, old story she had at one time known and then, later, almost forgotten. It was beautiful! Even more beautiful than in the books to hear it told by the schoolmistress with all the skill, all the eager youthfulness she infused into the telling. Luzina wanted to laugh, to cry.

"The first settlers were French. . . . The governor of Montreal, Maisonneuve. . . . His colleague at Quebec was called Champlain . . . the explorers of the New World, almost all of them, were French: Iberville, De Groseillers, Pierre Radisson. Father Marquette and Louis Joliet had discovered the water highway of the Great Lakes. La

Vérendrye had gone on foot as far as the Rockies. Cavelier de la Salle had travelled by boat to the mouth of the Mississippi. All this country belonged to France. . . . "

"The Water Hen, too?" asked Edmond.

"The Water Hen, too," the schoolmistress acquiesced, laughing.

Luzina likewise smiled indulgently.

Indeed yes, France was the mistress of the whole country! Like a good pupil, Luzina attentively followed the lesson, but she was, after all, far more advanced than the children; her memory, emancipated from household worries, liberated from almost all her life's history, dug up dates and certain battles which she rediscovered with delight. Even as she listened, Luzina had begun to spin on her own account the tale of the past.

Surely among those first settlers come from France there had been Tousignants, and people of her own family, the Bastiens. Luzina had been given to understand that the French colonists had been carefully picked; that no loafer or thief had been able to slip in amongst them. All good people. They had established themselves in what was formerly called Lower Canada and which was later to be included in the province of Quebec. The Tousignants and the Bastiens were of their number. Moreover, venturesome and courageous as Luzina for the moment saw them, some of those Lower Canada Tousignants and Bastiens had emigrated to the West, even as far as Manitoba. Already they were far, very far, from the places of their origin. But wait! said Luzina out loud. A Manitoba Bastien woman and a Manitoba Tousignant man had turned up who had in their blood the same tastes as their ancestors, *coureurs de bois* and *coureurs de plaine*. Nowadays you no longer went West, but there remained the North. No railways, no roads, almost no dwellings; they had been drawn to the North. No communications, no electricity, no schools – that had tempted them. Then again, how could you explain this folly, since no sooner were they settled in the North than they had set to work to make it

seem like other places! They had left villages fully established – she, Saint Jean Baptiste on the Red River, Hippolyte the fine village of Letellier – and ever since they had
toiled to transform the North, they had laboured to bring
there the customs, the atmosphere, the abundant life of
the South. Perhaps they were among those builders of
nations about whom Mademoiselle spoke with so much
warmth. Oh, if that were the case, Luzina could not bear
the glory of it without a few tears. Her eyes grew moist.
She could not endure listening to the all-too-beautiful
stories. Nor to the sad ones either. But it was the more
beautiful ones which finally played the greater havoc with
her heart. She crushed a little tear at the corner of a
swollen eyelid.

Ah, but wait a moment! To have come to the Water
Hen was not the best part of the story. The best part of it
was to have been rejoined, on the island in the Little
Water Hen, by the forebears, the former Tousignants, the
unknown Bastiens, Lower Canada, history, France, La
Vérendrye, Cavelier de la Salle. Luzina sniffled. That was
progress, far greater progress than the postman's aged
Ford, the store catalogues. What was she saying! For six
months of the year the winds might howl without slackening; the snow could shroud the house to its roof; and it
seemed as though the Tousignants on their island would
never again be alone.

"My cake!" thought Luzina.

She fled, angry at herself, blushing to the roots of her
hair and scattering shavings from her apron. What kind of
woman was she so to neglect her duty! To each his task in
life: to the teacher, the explaining; to the children, the
learning; and to her, Luzina, the serving of them all.

v

The afternoon seemed long to her. At half-past two,
school was adjourned for a recreation period. Luzina

moved to the threshold of the house, fully convinced that the children would come bounding to her to tell her about the progress they had made. At noon she had not, as it were, had time to question them, having been wholly busy with the vast preoccupation of making them absorb a double ration, since now they were working with their brains. She waited for them on the doorstep, touched and indulgent as if after a long absence. It seemed to her she had been bereft of her children for as long a while as when she used to leave them for her trips to Sainte Rose du Lac.

Like a whirlwind, the whole class dashed by, right under her nose. They all flew in Mademoiselle's wake. They reached a part of the island a little way off where there was a good piece of flat ground, there formed a circle, and began going through the motions of a game under the schoolmistress's leadership. The breeze carried to Luzina a few snatches of the old song Mademoiselle was singing: "*Savez-vous planter les choux . . . à la mode, à la mode et à la mode de par chez nous. . . .*" How charming they were, those civilized children's games, amidst the same old wanderings of the sheep, their tiresome laments, and the water hen's eternal chirping! Luzina moved forward a little the better to see them execute the round. She herself had sung and acted out the song in other days; she knew it well. You began by planting the cabbages with your hands. Then with the feet. You finished with your head, and that was the funniest of all. And sure enough, they were laughing a lot over there. Mademoiselle was showing how to plant cabbages with your nose. In their eagerness to imitate, the children were all shoving their noses into the soil and sticking their buttocks into the air. They laughed with joy. Mademoiselle was able to make them laugh as Luzina had never heard them laugh. Seemingly she knew how to get anything she wanted out of them. Thus she clapped her hands together, and at once they stood in line, very serious, intent on walking the way she did.

Oh, but just wait! said Luzina to herself. At four o'clock it will be another story. Little used to constraint, the children would welcome a return to the freer atmosphere of the house. And then they wouldn't be such angels. Mademoiselle herself would be worn out. Poor tiny Joséphine must be very wearied. Just wait for four o'clock! thought Luzina.

At four they wished each other good afternoon in the classroom, the teacher and the children, then they went out together, and in a moment all of them were in the house. It was almost like Luzina's homecoming from one of her trips, except that now it was her turn to ask questions.

"Did you learn a lot, Edmond? So you knew the name of the province, eh?"

Sure, he knew the name of the province; it wasn't hard to know the name of the province. Edmond even knew that there were nine provinces.

"You didn't stick your fingers in your nose?"

You didn't even talk about fingers in the nose before nice, pretty Mademoiselle!

"Have you begun to read, Joséphine?"

Yes, Joséphine almost knew how to read already. Joséphine had only two or three little things to learn, and she would be able to read all the books ever written. Joséphine was way ahead in her studies; Mademoiselle had said so. Their greatest worry was the fear of seeing their normal daily life revealed to Mademoiselle by some inept remark of their mother's. And then, too, they were afraid of seeing Mademoiselle disappear. You never knew, she might go for a walk, she might go off a long way, they might even lose sight of her. They all watched her, out of the corners of their eyes, ready to block her way. The moment she started to move, they clustered around her.

"Where are you going, Mademoiselle?"

Luzina intervened, her authority a bit tearful: "Now you let Mademoiselle alone. She's had enough of you."

Mademoiselle protested with a positiveness to match Luzina's exasperation: "Not at all! The children are so sweet. Let me have them a while longer, Madame Tousignant. We'll take a walk along the river bank. It will give me a chance to teach them something about things."

"Things? What next!"

"Yes, about birds, plants, insects," Mademoiselle explained.

"You're not going to keep on working twelve hours a day," complained Luzina.

"It's no more than a pleasure with such likable children," insisted the teacher.

"Likable! You don't know them," Luzina said. "They're perfect little devils."

The schoolmistress corrected her: "Nice children!"

How could the children disagree with a woman who described their true natures, their goodness of character, and whose keen insight located them at that high level of perfection she herself required of them!

"Hateful little brats!" complained Luzina. "If you begin to listen to them, they'll never leave you alone. Horrible children!"

"Good children," insisted Mademoiselle.

She hurried out. The children kept step with her as though they were all but a single person. Edmond left her side only when he ran a little ahead to pick some flower which he came back to offer her, bowing so low his forehead almost touched the ground.

"Thank you, Edmond; you are a thoughtful little boy."

She was explaining, "This must be mint. This, here, is wild mustard."

She knew all the things that children like to learn, the names of everything around them, the knowledge of which confers possession. Joséphine was trotting along behind the others, in her pink cotton dress, her stockings, and her best shoes.

Luzina's humbled authority fastened upon Joséphine who was unable to keep up with the others.

"Joséphine!" she cried out. "In any case, you're too small to learn about things. Come on back to the house! Do you hear?"

The child galloped all the faster, crestfallen, pretending not to hear.

"Joséphine!"

The little girl turned back. Her eyes were clouded. In the middle of the path, stamping her foot in anger at being delayed, she uttered her defiance: "The teacher said that I could learn about things too!"

What could she do? The little troop moved off into the rushes. Pierre held aside the higher stems, making a path for the young woman. The other children picked away the fluff from the dead bulrushes which kept sticking to her clothes; they kept brushing off her lovely suit. Out of breath, Joséphine cried out: "Mademoiselle, dear Mademoiselle, wait for Joséphine, wait for Joséphine!"

Now where on earth had they ever learned such loving thoughtfulness, a thoughtfulness they had never yet shown their own mother!

VI

The following summer there arrived on Little Water Hen island an amazing creature, prudish to excess, infatuated with hygiene, who had fixed ideas about everything; she was an Ontario old maid, speaking not a word of French, and a Protestant into the bargain.

She had bungled her whole trip north, and the journey had almost shattered her, especially that part of it spent in Nick Sluzick's bounding Ford; she was breathless when she entered the Tousignant house, and the moment she caught her breath, it was to begin her recriminations. It seemed almost impossible that so many grievances could find utterance at the same time.

Miss O'Rorke had been wronged by the government which had given her no proper idea of the trap into which she was to set foot and was not a bit troubled at seeing a "lady" travel alone through such country; principally she had been wronged by the bandits along the way. These bandits, whom she described as though they had been a horde, in the end turned out to consist of one solitary individual, Nick Sluzick. According to Miss O'Rorke, he had purposely driven her at hellish speed through the open prairie and over stumps and boulders. Inured to hardship, whenever she experienced it anew the poor woman no longer had any defence against this old acquaintance save to pretend that she had never before encountered it. Had she known what she would be up against before she left, she would never have set foot on the island in the Little Water Hen. She had been offered good posts in civilized regions. She could have had a big village school. And she would have turned right around and left had it not been so complicated. She supposed, however, that once in this Water Hen district, all she could do was stay there.

Having said her say, Miss O'Rorke removed a large hat pierced by several long pointed hairpins. She thus revealed a tired-looking bun of hair, a severe, sorrowful face and, behind dark-rimmed glasses, eyes expressive of a very dejected, very sad zeal, which were already ticking off the things that would have to be changed in the Tousignant household. At a glance she had discovered the water bucket, tidily covered with mosquito netting but furnished with a long-handled dipper from which everyone apparently drank, sticky flypapers cork-screwing down from the ceiling and, above all, that miserable, half-hidden little bed in the kitchen – if you please! Miss O'Rorke did not like promiscuity. And she was preparing herself very soon to ask for her own water glass.

"What's she saying?" whispered Luzina.

She had understood very little of the new arrival's talk. Hippolyte was thought to have the better knowledge of English.

"What did she say?" Luzina asked again, in a low tone.

Embarrassed at the thought of repeating such unamiable words before the person who had said them, Hippolyte urged his wife to have a little patience. "Later on you'll find out," said he with his eyes, and he looked deeply hurt.

"What do you think she is?" again whispered Luzina.

"She might well be Irish," Hippolyte answered without raising his voice.

"A Catholic, do you think?"

"Think not."

"What will the Capuchin Father say?" worried Luzina.

Yet, put out as Luzina was, she did not give up hope of making a friend, in the long run, of their "English-woman." Miss O'Rorke was thus labelled, for once and for all, in the minds of the Tousignants, young and old, since to them everyone who spoke English sprang from the same distant and completely foreign origin, and it would not have been possible to modify this classification even had it been proved that Miss O'Rorke's lineage had lived in Canada as long as the Bastiens and the Tousignants. But even a foreigner could be amiable. Anxious to be on good terms with everyone, Luzina attributed all kinds of qualities to people; according to her, it was impossible not to get along together if you wanted to. She had been friendly with Irish people, with Ruthenians, with French. Why could they not manage with their English-woman? She had a long row to hoe ahead of her.

Miss O'Rorke had never tested the wisdom of the old saying, "When in Rome, do as the Romans do." Her teacher's soul would rather have led her to attempt the transformation of the whole world rather than to abandon a single one of her set ideas and trifling whims. In the present circumstances, she had a particularly bad run of luck. A strict vegetarian, she was stranded on an island where salt pork was eaten from one end of the year to the other. She slept lightly. In order to sleep, she needed perfect silence around her. Now the ewes and their baby lambs roamed freely all over the island, and they were endlessly calling each other. Certain lambs, separated from their mothers at birth, bottle-fed, and kept a few days in the warmth of the kitchen, had acquired a taste for the house. When Miss O'Rorke could not sleep, she would relight her lamp; these lambs would then gather before her window, trustful of this tardy light; they would thrust their muzzles against the fly-screen and ask asylum. Toward dawn, when they finally grew quiet, the ducks and the water hens took over Miss O'Rorke's torment.

In the morning the poor woman's face was haggard. And what was most enraging of all to her mind was the fact that the Tousignants seemed astounded that she had been prevented from sleeping.

"You not sleep?" Luzina inquired with so much concern that it looked suspicious.

"Ah, too bad, very too bad!" said Luzina, truly upset.

They had not heard a sound. If anything could have disturbed their sleep it would have been precisely the unwonted, inexplicable quiet which the poor woman seemed to wish. In a land of sheep, what was extraordinary about hearing them bleat!

It was well worth while, Miss O'Rorke bitterly lamented, to come to the ends of the earth in order to discover that they did not even possess the only advantages you might have had a right to expect there – silence and peace! Luzina could not believe her ears. As for silence and peace, it did not seem possible to her that anywhere else could one have found them to so great an extent as along the Little Water Hen.

Finally, however, Miss O'Rorke became aware that the island was very long, and an amazing scheme entered her mind – a mind extraordinarily inventive the moment her comfort was in question. She told Hippolyte about this very simple discovery. Her idea was merely to exile the sheep to the other end of the island, seven miles away, and to build around the flock an enclosure sturdy enough to keep them there forever. In this way she would have peace.

Because she insisted on winning the schoolteacher by kindness, Hippolyte could not forgive Luzina for Miss O'Rorke's unreasonable requests. "That old fool of yours imagines that we're going to build a thousand feet of fence and travel the length of the island twice a day just to satisfy her little fancies."

With the old fool herself, however, he took a different tone. She overawed him with her glasses constantly directed toward him, and the way they reflected the glare of the sun troubled his eyes. What was more, Luzina had urged that they should continue to coax her with gentleness. "Try to win her by good manners," urged Luzina. "That's always the best policy in the end."

"Well?" asked the schoolmistress.

"Well," said Hippolyte, and he undertook to explain that he was not altogether master on Water Hen island. It belonged to the merchant Bessette, and Bessette could have had no other reason for establishing his ranch on an empty island at the edge of nowhere than that there he would be freed of the necessity of raising fences. Fences were expensive, and Bessette had one thoroughly fixed principle: the least expense possible, the most profit possible.

"You see?" inquired Hippolyte.

But out of all this the old maid principally gathered that a man named Bessette was responsible for the noise which disturbed her sleep. She set to work to write him a few well chosen words on the subject. There was no effort too troublesome for Miss O'Rorke once she had determined to change some little thing in this world where just about everything annoyed her.

Meanwhile it was discouraging to Luzina to see her refuse, at every meal, the salt pork, the red cabbage with vinegar, and the pancakes.

"Don't you like?" said Luzina, sincerely sympathetic; yet to speak English to an Englishwoman was torture to her, and when she was tortured, Luzina always had a desire to laugh.

When the worst of the heat was over, she conceived the idea of sending to Rorketon for a piece of fresh meat. The government had entrusted to her the task of extending hospitality to the schoolmistress, and she had no intention of shirking that task. She busied herself with settling, two weeks in advance, the itinerary of the meat, this being more difficult than it would have been in the case of a human being who could change vehicles under his own power.

Luzina ordered her meat by mail. At the same time she had to inform Ivan Bratislovski, also by mail, that he would have to pick up the meat at the butcher's, but only at the very last minute, so as to give the said meat a chance to remain as long as possible on ice; urge Nick Sluzick not to forget to ask his colleague Bratislovski for the piece of beef, since the latter was absent-minded and might very well take it back with him to Rorketon (this very thing had happened during the Capuchin Father's last visit); finally, remind both postmen to keep the beef well wrapped to protect it from the flies and extreme heat, not to put it in the mail bags, and not to sit on it.

Despite all these precautions, either because some of them were neglected along the way or because they were themselves insufficient, the piece of beef arrived in precarious condition. It was too bad; you could see at a glance that it would have made a fine roast. Luzina hoped in any case to disguise its odour with a good spice sauce. Miss O'Rorke must have had a refined palate and sense of smell; at the very first mouthful she made a face.

Hippolyte, little given to laughter, by nature indeed serious and humourless, for some reason or other found this business of the roast beef exceptionally funny; Luzina's three letters, the stages of the journey worked out in advance like a railway timetable, the ill humour of Sluzick, who above all else detested taking charge of fresh meat in midsummer, all these elaborate negotiations leading to nothing more than their Englishwoman's expression of martyrdom!

He burst out laughing. The embarrassment of hearing himself laugh in the midst of complete silence made Hippolyte laugh even harder. The eyes of all the astounded children shuttled from their father to poor Miss O'Rorke. Luzina had threatened them with at least ten punishments for every breach of the respect they owed their teacher. Here and there, hesitant little chuckles began and were choked off. Suddenly Luzina herself let go her own irresistible wild laughter. Then all of them broke down. For fully five minutes, the Tousignants, freed of a long constraint, laughed their heads off at Miss O'Rorke who, very stiff, her lips pursed, crumbled a bit of bread while sighing for the day when she would at last shake the dust of this island from her feet.

Once the crisis was over, Luzina begged everyone not to let it happen again. "Perhaps she suspected we were laughing at her," said Luzina with a glance of obvious repentance at Miss O'Rorke.

In one way it was rather convenient that the teacher did not understand French. Luzina could, in her presence, give vent to lessons in politeness as direct and concrete as they possibly could be. "You can see perfectly well that she looks out of sorts. Do try not to stare at her. We don't know what may be on her mind from time to time."

Out of delicacy, nevertheless, when Luzina said such things, she looked elsewhere, usually at a religious calendar. Thus the poor woman had learned to recognize the occasions when the talk was about her and to associate them with Saint Joseph, for whom she already cherished no love whatever. These likable and kindly Tousignants were, of all the people she had ever undertaken to rescue from ignorance, the most stiff-necked.

Every morning there were protestations and tears. The children did not want to go to school. Miss O'Rorke the whole day long addressed them with patriotic speeches which they did not understand, and she was incensed because they had not grasped her comments. She called them "ungrateful children, very ungrateful children." According to her, the government could not be worse repaid for its kindness than by this Tousignant family; generously treated as it was by an English government, it intended to remain French. Where could you find anything worse in the line of ingratitude? "The government is English, the province is English," Miss O'Rorke tirelessly explained; "you should conform to the majority and the general will." Two or three of the pupils tried to run away from school every morning. Luzina had a job on her hands to recapture them. But she persevered. Education could be nothing other than a joy. Such great riches, so deep an experience might well warrant a few tears. She reasoned with the children: "Now, last summer you learned French with Mademoiselle Côté. This year, learn English; take advantage of it to learn English."

At bottom a great opportunist, Luzina at last discovered one merit in her Englishwoman: that was the English language. Although incapable herself of savouring it, Luzina held it to be no less a merit. If anyone had something to say against Miss O'Rorke, Luzina found an excuse for it: "Anyhow, she speaks English well."

Miss O'Rorke, however, possessed another, more meritorious virtue, although it was to remain substantially invisible to the Tousignants. Miss O'Rorke's heart, lonely and none too amiable, throbbed with an excessive loyalty to the British Empire, and especially to the United Kingdom, with the exception of Catholic Ireland, where she had never set foot. Fired by a passion fully as unreasonable, Mademoiselle Côté had caused its extravagances to blossom around her; Mademoiselle Côté had left as her legacy the names of personages as far from the Tousignants as the moon. Cavelier de la Salle, La Vérendrye, Radisson, Frontenac, the evil Intendant Bigot – all of them, even the bad ones, had a right to faithful remembrance. Perhaps Mademoiselle Côté retained the advantage of having been the first to come to the island. What opportunity to stimulate their imaginations could Miss O'Rorke find in her Act of Capitulation, in the French defeat, in her Fathers of Confederation and her Dominion of Canada? What was more, she was imprudent enough to attack Mademoiselle Côté's heroes. The English General

Wolfe, according to her, had soundly beaten Mademoiselle Côté's Montcalm who, Frenchman that he was, had gone to battle with lace frills on his shirt and had politely offered his enemy the first volley.

But it is impossible completely to withstand even an inept passion, and Miss O'Rorke's for the British Isles finally won her a small victory over the Tousignants.

VII

About two months and a half after her arrival, Miss O'Rorke was taking her Sunday stroll toward the end of the island where the sedges were thickest. She had got into the habit of mitigating her boredom by long solitary walks, which sometimes took her to the island's northern tip, the spot to which she had hoped to banish the flock of sheep and, failing in this, where she had intended to pitch a tent that she could herself use as a retreat. Like the first, this scheme had fallen through; confronted by Miss O'Rorke's announcement of her odd resolve, Luzina had begun to whimper, truly provoked and alarmed.

"What would people say? People would certainly talk."

"People! What people?" Miss O'Rorke had inquired; she now was beginning to learn a little French, based on Luzina's vivid vocabulary.

Unable to say exactly what people she had in mind, Luzina was still just as afraid of talk.

"People will say that we have mistreated you, and they will blame us."

And thus the last advantage by which Miss O'Rorke had hoped to benefit from her stay on Little Water Hen island slipped from her grasp. Here there was no solitude. Of course, the poor woman reflected, human beings and animals, when they are unfortunate enough to live in what is practically a wilderness, are condemned to living very close together. So that Sunday she set forth, her back turned on the four cabins. The clouds floated vaguely across the sky, slow to overtake each other, and the Big Water Hen, itself lazy and unruffled, reflected the clouds' continuous procession. The sheep, as sometimes happened with them, had of their own choice and in one solid mass emigrated toward the island's distant tip. There was almost nothing to ruffle Miss O'Rorke's calm. Here was one of those quiet, drowsy days when the island really seemed to be uninhabited. And then it burst upon Miss O'Rorke that there was no flag floating over the island. She must have been distracted indeed not to have noticed it before. She went back by the shortest possible route and stepped firmly into the kitchen.

"Mrs Tousignant, there must be a flag here."

"What is she asking?" Luzina sought enlightenment from her husband.

"Now she wants a flag!" Hippolyte interpreted.

"A flag!" Luzina exclaimed with great affability. "True enough, we need a flag. But what sort of flag?"

"The flag of His Majesty the King," said Miss O'Rorke.

Luzina fastened on the word majesty. As far as British majesty was concerned, Luzina was rather behind the times; in this matter she had progressed no further than the old Queen Victoria, whom she respected because, Protestant though Victoria had been, she had borne nine children. To Luzina, large families seemed a purely Catholic obligation, which was not to be shirked since Heaven depended upon it. Victoria, who was not bound by such requirements, seemed to her all the more meritorious. It was as though Victoria had acted as she had only to set a good example and perhaps to comfort the other women of her Empire.

Eager to please, Luzina tore an old worn sheet into strips. These she dyed and assembled under the schoolmistress's instructions. So proud was she of her Union Jack that she would gladly have sewn a few others, now that she had the pattern. Meanwhile Miss O'Rorke had begun to plague Hippolyte. Seemingly it was not enough to have a Union Jack; it must be able to flutter freely in

the breeze, firmly planted in front of the school and visible
from all directions. Stimulated by the symbol of Empire,
Miss O'Rorke had found fresh energy. Ultimately Hippolyte understood that the Englishwoman wanted a flagpole.
Truth to tell, Hippolyte deliberately took a long time to
understand Miss O'Rorke's wishes. Luzina and the children were vastly more interested in the flag. Beyond question it would help to define an area which otherwise might
have passed for unexplored. Pierre-Emmanuel-Roger, following the teacher's specifications, trimmed a pole eight
feet long. But then a difficulty arose; according to Miss
O'Rorke, it was necessary to hoist the flag every morning
when school opened and to lower it at the stroke of four.
Hippolyte could not see why, once the flag was installed at
the tip of the pole, it should not remain there indefinitely.
Less stubborn, Luzina sewed a deep hem along one of the
flag's edges. Pierre threaded a line through this hem; then
he climbed the pole and affixed the line in such fashion
that, depending on which end of the line you pulled, the
Union Jack slipped to the top of the mast, came down,
went up again. The hoisting and lowering of the flag could
all be managed from below; it was no trouble to put the
flag at half-mast or to raise it into the wind's full force, for
the fun of seeing it whip and snap. They had at hand all
that was needed to betoken mourning, holidays, days of
rejoicing, of toil, of departure. In her own fashion Miss
O'Rorke left her mark on the island.

One autumn afternoon, toward the end of October,
they went to turn her back to Nick Sluzick. Despite the
diversion supplied by the business of the flag, Luzina was
not too upset at seeing the Englishwoman go. Just as they
reached the mainland, the postman's Ford came bouncing
along the river's edge. It continued without slackening
speed, passing the little mound, slightly levelled off at the
top which, according to conventions unwritten but of long
standing, represented the stopping point of their common
carrier. They could see the mailman's heavy hands firmly
grasping the wheel. His face danced up and down; his

moustaches quivered; Nick Sluzick was dashing along as he used to in the old days when there was no one to pick up along the trail. As one the Tousignants raised their arms; Hippolyte whistled. At last the old fellow came to a stop, but a good way off, in the middle of a muddy pool which had not yet fully dried out.

He had a quick eye. No one could accuse Nick Sluzick of not seeing the people who waited for him in the midst of this bare country. At a glance Nick had even recognized, in this exceedingly visible group, the woman traveller of last spring who had endlessly implored him to watch where he was going. As though Nick Sluzick needed someone to guide him over these roads he had navigated these past twelve years, the only man who could master them! Nick sat squarely on the centre of the front seat; the back seat was covered with mail bags and large packages. Miss O'Rorke had to accept the narrow space beside him which the motionless postman neither offered nor refused. Nick Sluzick remained superbly aloof from what was going to happen.

At the Ford's first bound the mail bags, piled up to the coarse canvas top, lost their equilibrium and began to tumble down toward Miss O'Rorke. She received their full impact upon her shoulders. Her hat went askew, and her glasses almost shot out of the car.

The unfortunate old maid was leaving, and without much feeling of relief after all. It would be no better elsewhere. For twenty-five years she had been knocking about, from job to job, and the next one in line was always a little more remote, a little deeper in the wilderness; the food was heavier and heavier, sentiments less and less refined, gratitude rarer and rarer. This post on the Little Water Hen had perhaps, all in all, not been too disagreeable. At a venture, unable to risk making a movement or even turning her head to look, because of the mail bags which weighed against her neck, Miss O'Rorke waved one hand outside the Ford, in the Tousignants' general direction.

Whenever she quit a place, in fact, she had a fairly painful time of it. With amazement she became aware that life had not been too bad in the spot she was leaving. It even seemed to her moderately pleasant. And finally she would come to believe that in that place alone existence would have been possible for her. Such was Miss O'Rorke. Her preference – gloomy and depressing – always was given to that which she had lost, and if there were crannies in this world which she lauded without respite, they were always those where she was certain never again to set foot.

Different though her nature was, Luzina nonetheless found certain people more likable at departure than upon arrival. Her Englishwoman – so unpredictable, eccentric, and disconcerting – at the moment of her going became one more friend for her in this oversized, inadequately peopled world where, Luzina felt, you never could have too many friends.

Returning in Indian file, thoughts of Miss O'Rorke did not lessen the Tousignants' curiosity about their next teacher. Luzina brought up the rear, out of breath despite the briskness of the weather, her cheeks red, she herself a trifle saddened by the void Miss O'Rorke left behind her, but her eyes smiling at the thought of the new schoolmistress who would take her place. She had reached the conclusion that they would never have the same teacher two years running; in a way this pleased her appetite for novelty. The great differences she had glimpsed in teaching methods as between only two schoolmistresses opened to her a vast field for conjecture. Without being aware of it, the whole family had already acquired a taste for living in suspense during the longer half of the year, busy thinking about what kind of teacher they would have next, as might some remote colony awaiting the arrival of its new governor. Change suited them. It added zest to life, afforded subject matter for long winter's conversations. "Perhaps she'll be a Hungarian," Luzina remarked one fine day. No one knew what could have given Luzina such an idea, but they all knew that Luzina had been thinking of the new schoolmistress. This attraction toward the unknown in their existence prevented too keen feelings of regret; to some extent it even militated against loyalty. "Certainly we'd be pleased if Mademoiselle Côté were to come again – no doubt of that," Luzina would say, yet at the same time she had an inkling that her heart would not welcome such a return. Of course it would be very nice to see Mademoiselle Côté once more, but not at the cost of missing a new teacher, still unknown to them, whom they were beginning to feel they could not forgo, at least until they had had a chance to know her.

By spring Luzina had exhausted all the possibilities. Their schoolmistress had appeared to her mind's eye in the guise of almost every nationality. She thought she had prepared herself for any possible surprise. Only one had she forgotten. The schoolmistress who arrived at the island early in May turned out to be a young man.

VIII

This young man landed on the island clad, at least, in appropriate garb. Luzina even thought it a bit exaggerated. She saw advancing toward her an odd silhouette topped with a colonial helmet, wearing a red-checked flannel shirt and heavy oiled boots; he was laden with an armoury of weapons, rifles large and small. From his shoulder hung a game bag; to his back was attached a blanket roll. Surveyors off for a full three or four months' trip in trackless wilderness would have carried no more equipment. Luzina had another reason for being ill at ease; she was five months gone with child and, under the circumstances, she found unbecoming the presence of a young man who could daily watch her girth increase. It had been embarrassing enough to submit to Miss O'Rorke's constant examination from behind her spectacles, and Miss O'Rorke had had no reason for alarm, because that summer Luzina was taking a rest.

He was a likable chap, however, without pretence, and seemingly at once pleased with the island. No glance he cast at Luzina hinted that he was curious as to whether she were fatter or more rotund than usual. Luzina would have found him wholly to her taste had he only shown as much interest in the schoolroom as he did in the chase.

He would ask Luzina to leave him a little coffee in the pot; he would then get up while it was still dark, help himself, and, presumably, find his way out into the rushes, since from the house where everyone was asleep you could hear the whistle of bullets in that direction. This was the hour when the little water hens, the terns, the ducks – creatures that took delight in the pale glow of dawn – were rousing. The sun would come up, the shooting cease. And yet the schoolmaster would not return. The children, seated at their small desks, would sometimes wait for him until ten o'clock, having long since finished the lessons he had indicated on the blackboard. What on earth could the teacher be doing? One morning Luzina sent out a search party in her anxiety. Here is what the children discovered: their instructor lay asleep, stretched out on a flat-bottomed boat among the reeds, with his cap over his face to protect him from the flies and sun.

His teaching methods, moreover, were vastly curious. He gave the impression of considering the whole business a huge joke. "Learn what's on this page if you feel like it," he would say with a laugh, and he seemed to be slyly telling them. "Don't learn it if you are no more tempted to than I am tempted to teach you."

Luzina's children, however, were bent on learning.

Every evening each would seek out his nook and declaim for hours on end, this one a grammatical rule, that one a historical passage; and, in order to hear themselves, they would all yell louder and louder as time went on. Joséphine's voice was particularly ear-splitting. All this did not displease Luzina; it gave her, rather, the impression that her children were making great progress. But when they proudly informed their teacher that they "knew their lesson," Armand Dubreuil would begin to laugh. "Well, then, since you're so quick at it, get to work on the next page!"

To hear him talk, you would think the most intelligent course was adroitly to escape effort. After the passage of a few weeks, rather than making up the school hours of which he had cheated the children in the morning, Armand Dubreuil robbed them of another at the end of the day. At three o'clock, class was dismissed. Then, with his gun under his arm, he would disappear deep into the wooded part of the island. The prairie chickens' outcries made it clear that it was to them he was giving his attention. They fluttered over the ground or else ran for a bit, their bodies rolling comically on their spindly legs, almost as fat and awkward as barnyard hens. Bing! Bing! For hours you could hear the popping of the twenty-two rifle.

Evenings he would tell stories. He had quickly acquired Hippolyte's trick of sitting back on his heels and rocking to and fro while he smoked his pipe. From day to day Luzina postponed the remarks which she thought it her duty to address to him; it was very difficult; Armand Dubreuil was such a pleasant fellow. He was easygoing; you might have thought that he had always lived with them. He developed an interest in sheep raising; he would calculate the profits which would have been theirs had they been the owners of the hundred and fifty sheep. He was keen about everything except his school. Luzina sought for ways of remonstrating with him without hurting his feelings. Thereupon he would give the children a whole day off, alleging as excuse some holiday of which Luzina could find no mention whatever on the calendar. Miss O'Rorke's flag was far too often at half-mast. At last Luzina thought she had found a way to reprimand the teacher without irritating him. She began praising Mademoiselle Côté to the skies.

"That schoolmistress we had year before last – Lord! did

she stick to her job! Do you remember, children, the lovely gold stars she would give you! With her, school started at nine on the dot. Nice, attractive, but my! what a hard worker! She had found the children way behind in their studies. To make up for lost time, she even had school on Saturdays!"

Armand Dubreuil laughed wholeheartedly. "My method is different," said he. "I don't believe in forcing children too much. Nature, you understand, is still the best teacher. Nature teaches us more than all the books. But it takes years to see the fruits of my method. Nature – that's my system. And it's the best."

Such was not at all Luzina's view of the matter. They had nature in plenty all around them; there would always be enough of that. Yet how could she discuss pedagogy with an educated young man who had an answer for everything and whom she was afraid of offending? She was made even more impotent when one day Armand Dubreuil artlessly began to call her Mama Tousignant. He knew her weak spot. The salt pork, the pancakes, the game stews – everything Luzina concocted – seemed excellent to him: "I've never eaten as well as in your house, Mama Tousignant. Do make me another cup of your fine coffee, Mama Tousignant."

Luzina complained to Hippolyte: "He's such a coaxer; he twists me around his little finger and I can't be as severe as I should."

Hippolyte likewise was worried, but for another reason. Never had such carnage been seen upon their island. Occasionally they had killed, for eating purposes, a wild duck or a fine prairie chicken, well fattened and fully grown. Never had they shot for the sake of mere practice. Now the schoolteacher was a good shot, and he should have been satisfied long since at the proof he had given of that fact. He continued to kill indiscriminately: water hens whose coarse flesh was scarcely edible; an unfortunate bittern, which had found asylum a few days earlier in one of the coves of the Little Water Hen, a long-shanked, melancholy, lonely bird that had shattered the air with its booming; and female ducks, almost certainly.

The hunting season had not yet begun, and Hippolyte feared difficulties with the government. In no case did he like trouble with the authorities, especially not now when they were in such official favour. They had received personal letters from the government. Luzina, you might say, was in direct and constant touch with the government. Now, less than ever, was law-breaking in order. Bessette might report them to the Mounted Police, were he to think that he could thus succeed in closing the school. Hippolyte was deeply upset. Yet he had not the courage, either, openly to reprimand education personified. If anyone knew the law, it should have been the schoolmaster.

One evening he expressed what he had to say in a wholly tactful fashion. "Mother, when does the hunting season open?" Hippolyte inquired.

Astounded, Luzina replied, "But you know very well Father; the season begins about September eighteenth."

"Yes, that's just what I thought," said Hippolyte. "I've been telling myself, these last few days, that the hunting season doesn't begin until the eighteenth of September. We're in July. So we have a good two months before hunting begins."

Armand Dubreuil was far from obtuse. Hippolyte's little stratagem made him laugh even harder than Luzina's reproaches. Sitting on the floor with his back to the wall and his short pipe between his teeth, he expounded to them his view of the law. "Can you people see any government inspector arriving on Little Water Hen island! You'd first of all have to go get him, show him the way, drag him out of swamps, lead by the hand. Give him a rub-down, encourage him with hot toddies . . . "

Hippolyte was afraid of expressing too direct a rebuke and went off to take a stroll along the shore of the Big Water Hen. At its middle the river ran free; outside the current it was encumbered with sedges. They spread everywhere, gaining ground from year to year, just as did the crops elsewhere, the tilth, the forest – a country really made for the birds. Each spring they came from the depths of Florida, two thousand miles as a bird flies, hastening and following a cunning course in order to reach this sure asylum! Perhaps more than two thousand miles! The mother birds must have remembered the water which came halfway up the length of the rushes. Here were the finest hiding-places in the world in which to have their ducklings when first they began to swim, and then to show them how to fly from tuft to tuft. Hippolyte sighed heavily. He did not like to see young lives snuffed out before they had even learned to suspect danger. He did not like to see mothers snatched away from their broods. And to think of that long journey of confidence, from the depths of Florida, ending in disaster!

By now, however, it was very late in the day to become annoyed at Armand Dubreuil. He made himself increasingly at home with the Tousignants. To his heart's content he practised a more and more extraordinary teaching method – laughter, indulgence, liberty. "There is nothing like liberty," he would say. "Why push the children so much? They'll always know as much as they need to. What good do you suppose grammar and history will do them in these parts?"

"Aren't you happy here?" he would then ask.

Certainly they were happy, but what had that to do with their little knowledge?

Inclined as she was to look at the pleasant side of things, Luzina could not help realizing that, as far as education was concerned, they were going from bad to worse. In the end, perhaps, all they would have would be someone who came to the island in the Little Water Hen to spend a pleasant holiday.

Yet at the beginning of August it began to rain, and Armand Dubreuil, unable to indulge his favourite pastime, had to fall back on his schoolwork. He began abruptly to be almost as zealous in its behalf as he had been about hunting. Everyone then could see what precious things he had denied his pupils by his earlier neglect of duty. Invariably he translated arithmetic problems into terms of sheep, and thus every calculation became a matter of immediate interest to all of them, and they all laboured at its solution. He asked Luzina for a great variety of disparate objects: a perfectly spherical tomato, another smaller tomato, clothespins, and thread; then, with the help of these things, he showed that the earth was round, that it revolved on its axis wrapped in its threads of latitude and longitude and in the effulgence from the other tomato, which also revolved and was the sun. In this fashion the children understood what Luzina had already maintained: that it was night on one portion of the terrestrial globe while elsewhere the sun was shining. He was a good teacher – even an excellent teacher.

In the evening he sat in the kitchen with a book, very different in this respect from Miss O'Rorke, who locked herself up and even shoved a table against the door and seemed unable to erect enough barriers to protect her pathetic privacy, which was ever lacking something. The sight of an open book, of a person absorbed in reading, had always been soothing and alluring to Luzina. She asked the teacher if what he were reading was very interesting. It continued to rain, a heavy rain which beat down on the roof of the house. Armand Dubreuil began reading aloud the fictionalized account of a visit to the North Pole. And the Tousignant family, on the very edge of the inhabited world, lost all feeling of isolation in its enthralled concern for the sufferings, the cold, the loneliness endured by these imaginary personages.

Luzina was overwhelmed. She who so readily commiserated real misfortune, how could she fail to be stirred by the mishaps which novelists are so skilled at piling upon the backs of their creatures! The worst was that the moment one catastrophe had been averted, another began to threaten. Luzina was continuously afraid for the explorers on their perilous expedition. Yet it never would have occurred to her to spare her emotions by putting a stop to the reading. On the contrary, the more calamities there were to dread, the more eager she was to hear about them. Never would she have believed that you could be at once so happy and so anxious. The rain whipped at the windows. The reader's voice drowned out the gusts. The stove, barely alight, emitted a little warmth. They felt themselves secure, and their hearts contracted at the thought that others were in a different case. With tears in her eyes, Luzina begged, "A little more, Monsieur Dubreuil; let us at least learn how they find their way through the storm!"

She could not resign herself to the tepid comfort of bed while at that very moment the explorers were wandering lost.

Occasionally, as though the reader had some power of intercession with the author and could rescue Luzina's heroes from their discomfiture, she threatened the teacher: "Come, now! Don't you dare let another of them perish!"

After the odyssey of these explorers, not one of whom survived, Armand Dubreuil read the true and tragic adventures of forty convicts exiled to Siberia.

How cold and inhuman a spot was that Siberia! How far away! What hardhearted Czars were those Nicholases, Emperors of all the Russias! Luzina no longer heard the wind thrust at her own door or the coyotes howling at the full moon not very far from where she sat. She thanked Heaven she was in Canada, in a country civilized, well governed, and progressive. Even though she considered the characters in books quite as real as she was herself, not at all inventions of their authors' minds, Luzina blessed the talent that must have been necessary to make all this living thing vivid and clear. "Don't leave us hungry for more, Monsieur Dubreuil!"

He was completely transformed. As though to make up for lost time, he fed them double rations. The children never could complete the homework outlined for them on the blackboard. Joséphine alone held up in this marathon he had devised for them. Grammar, arithmetic, geogra-

phy – everything at breakneck speed. Edmond had night-
mares. They rushed from page to page without catching
breath; hardly ever did the schoolmaster give them an
hour's recreation. Everything he did he had to do to
excess. All the same, Luzina had no intention of reproach-
ing him now for this sudden zeal. Perhaps he was moved
by remorse. Or else, as always, Luzina's formula of winning people with honey was at last bearing fruit.

Then Luzina brusquely awakened to the truth. One
evening as he closed his book, Armand Dubreuil calmly
announced that he was leaving the next day.

It was only the end of August; the schoolmaster was
engaged until the end of October. The large box he had
brought with him and which Luzina now knew was
packed with books was far from having been emptied.
Luzina was about to protest when, of a sudden, she wondered whether this were not some new form of teasing on
his part; he was a great wag.

"You're not serious in your talk about leaving; you're
trying to frighten us," she asserted.

He assumed an air of amusement. "All the same, I've a
fine school in the South. A school with three grades,
located in a large village. You wouldn't want to have me
miss a chance of advancing myself, would you, Mama
Tousignant?"

The next day she got up very early and found him
already rigged in the same fashion as on his arrival, his
blanket on his back, his rifles over his shoulder. He was
adjusting under his chin the strap of his pith helmet.
Luzina felt he was carrying the joke a little too far. "Why
are you upsetting us this way, Monsieur Dubreuil?"

He laughed again. "There's no time to fool around if I
want to catch old Sluzick."

She began brewing him some coffee; she still hesitated
to believe him. "We're only in August; you could at least
stay on until October. All this nonsense is just some more
of your practical joking. . . . And the best hunting of all is
in autumn." She hoped that that would lure him.

"Too bad, too bad! But my school in the South begins on the fourth of September. A school built of brick, if you please, and what's more, Mama Tousignant, your little Dubreuil has been appointed its principal."

He swallowed the last mouthfuls of coffee and moved toward her, smiling, teasing, his hand outstretched. "Many thanks and good-bye, Mama Tousignant."

So it was true that he was leaving. To have been doubtful of it to the end made his departure all the harder. She had slept in peace; had she bestirred herself, perhaps she might have been able to keep him a bit longer.

"So soon! Already! Almost without giving us time to see you go!"

He had not always been conscientious, at least during the beginning of his stay. He had advocated bad principles – nature, indulgence, freedom. Yet perhaps he had been the best teacher of all. Henceforward they never would be able to see a tomato without remembering that the earth is round. Truly an odd master! He had said that it was not very important to learn, and yet it was he who had given them the strongest taste for it.

"Won't you come back?" Luzina asked. "Do try next summer!"

She had grown used to mothering him. She had mended his hunting trousers, often torn when he came home from the willow and hazelnut thickets. She had washed and ironed his shirts, kept cleaning his pipe ashes everywhere he went. Neither with Mademoiselle Côté, who was very fastidious, nor with Miss O'Rorke, who was grimly independent, had Luzina enjoyed these small pleasures. Above all it had been the schoolmaster's contentment at living with them which had won him Luzina's heart.

"We'll expect you next year."

"I've been appointed principal," he began again. "You understand, Mama Tousignant, I'm quite a learned fellow. I have my bachelor's degree."

She opened her eyes wide, without fully understanding what it was all about except that here was a further reason for hanging onto the teacher. Now, however, he left all seriousness behind. "Good-bye freedom!" said he. "I'm a real fool! One hundred and fifty dollars a month, Principal Dubreuil. . . . I'm slipping my head into the noose. . . . Not a particle of all that is worth a single day on the island in the Little Water Hen!"

As he moved away, he turned and fixed his eyes on the small building Hippolyte had erected for the future and for knowledge.

What would be the outcome of all this? A great deal of sorrow, perhaps, for Mama Tousignant. What, indeed, would come of it? Discontent first of all, which lies at the root of all progress? And afterward?

"Would you like my advice, Mama Tousignant?" he inquired, still laughing but a trifle more serious than usual. "Close your school. You'll never get anything here except old battle-axes like your Miss O'Rorke or fellows like me who come because they want to hunt. And eventually you won't even see the likes of us. In the end, summer classes attract only misfits, and from what I hear that species is dying in our profession."

He saluted her, with two fingers touching the visor of his helmet. He preferred leaving alone, with Pierre as his only companion, he being needed to bring the boats back to the near shores of the two rivers. He knew how to get along by himself. The countryside had become familiar to him, intimate, easy, like some way of life a man at first glance knows would fully content him and on which, for that very reason, he turns his back. If this happiness were not so easy, would you thus casually leave it behind, calmly and whistling some little tune?

"Monsieur Dubreuil!" Luzina called him back.

He was already at some distance, ready to take his seat in the boat. He put his hand to his ear, made a sign that he was listening. She cried out into the wind, "Come back, one of these days!"

She was far from understanding this last lesson he had sought to teach her, more ambiguous than all the others.

But he had left alone, as he had wanted, when he had wanted. He had himself taken up the oars. It was as though one of themselves were leaving, and Luzina's heart was touched with anxiety. During the course of the winter she constrained herself not to think too much out loud of the teacher to come, and she did this out of prudence, in the hope, probably, of extracting from the future something even better by demanding little. Whoever might wish to come to the Little Water Hen would be well received and duly appreciated.

But the following summer no one came to the island.

IX

You might have doubted the existence of the English kings Miss O'Rorke had introduced into the island, and Mademoiselle Côté's heroes, however far afield they had planted the flag of France, and even Dubreuil's unhappy exiles, had it not been that the tiny schoolhouse remained. After its fashion it gave witness to a civilization which would have existed. A traveller coming to the island and seeing there one cabin more than was strictly needed by its population might have meditated on the tale it told of progress and decline. The little structure leaned at an angle; the bitter cold had wrenched its joints, and on one side it had sunk perceptibly. A pair of squirrels had succeeded in forcing an entrance between two logs which had pulled a trifle apart. On the blackboard you could decipher, as in truncated messages from the distant past, a few scraps of Armand Dubreuil's last lesson: "Nouns ... *al* ... in the plural ... cept *bal*, *chacal* ... " The brush had obliterated the rest. The map of the world was hanging askew.

Luzina had several times remarked, "We mustn't let the school go to wrack and ruin." Yet one day, not knowing where to stow away a bag of grain, Hippolyte had leaned it against a corner of the schoolroom. Pierre used it to store his fishing apparatus. Wolf traps were hung up there. The school was in process of becoming a lumber room. And the summer ran its course like the Water Hen itself, sleepy amidst its rushes. No longer was it necessary to wash every morning, and why wear shoes now? Pierre gave up his books. Often had he been humiliated and provoked; in school he had felt very backward for his age. Now he was relieved at last to be able to devote himself, a man full-fledged and unharassed, to the important business of life – the sheep, fishing, firewood. Meanwhile Joséphine had become schoolmistress on Little Water Hen island. She would lead a row of four or five small Tousignants into a corner of the kitchen or outdoors under a birch tree, and she would announce, with a serious mien strangely reminiscent of Mademoiselle Côté: "School will now begin." Then she would insist that they greet each other politely.

Luzina's heart swelled at seeing the children repeat last year's lessons from morning until night. And as though to embitter her regrets, the Department of Education continued to send pamphlets and communications of one sort or another. The government people seemed unaware that the Little Water Hen school was closed. Other blackboard erasers arrived, and then a packet of letters from New Zealand children forwarded through the courtesy of a Miss Patterson of the Department. This consisted of answers to letters written two years earlier by the Tousignant children under Miss O'Rorke's direction. In order to create and maintain cordial relations between the various subjects of the British throne, Miss O'Rorke required the pupils in every school through which she passed to write letters to their small cousins in South Africa, Australia, Newfoundland, or some other portion of the Empire "on which the sun never set."

That summer the Tousignants still received a magazine published by the Department of Education. Luzina was leafing it through one morning when abruptly she gave an exclamation of shock and pride. The letter Edmond had written two years ago to a little New Zealand friend was there before Luzina's eyes, in the full dignity of print. It was headed, "A Water Hen District Student Describes His Life for Us."

Luzina remembered Edmond's letter very well. Into it Miss O'Rorke had injected many ideas of her own, especially toward the end, where she had Edmond say that he was happy to belong to a great Empire. She had of course helped with spelling and punctuation. All the same, a number of the short sentences were wholly Edmond's. A greater friend of originality than one might have imagined, Miss O'Rorke had respected their un-English way of saying things. Luzina unravelled some part of it.

"I am at the Little Water Hen. My mother is Mrs Tousignant. My father keeps Bessette's sheep. One has a hundred and forty-nine sheep. One is far from the big train. Never in all my life have I taken the big train. But my mother takes the big train. She gets babies. And how do you like New Zealand, you, my little New Zealand friend? Have you sheep? I like New Zealand. Do send me your photograph. I'll send you my photograph if I have one. I have another little new baby. One has a lot of babies. Have you a baby?"

And it was signed in full, Rosario-Lorenzo-Edmond Tousignant.

"Heaven's sake! Heaven's sake!" Luzina was in an ecstasy.

Edmond's friend's answer appeared on the same page, and had as title, "A Few Words from Bill McEwan."

More fortunate than Edmond, Bill McEwan had his picture in the magazine; it had been taken near his home, in a clearing amidst huge trees, and showed him leaning against a small plank structure. Apparently this New Zealand was rather similar to the Little Water Hen; he also mentioned sheep.

Luzina ran off to find Hippolyte in the sheepfold. She was waving the paper in the air. "Edmond's letter!"

What was Luzina talking about! To the best of Hippolyte's knowledge, Edmond had not left, so why the talk about letters? Luzina spread the open pages before Hippolyte's eyes. He was busy. With his hands he continued to take care of a sick lamb. He began reading a few words. "I am at the Little Water Hen. My father keeps Bessette's sheep. . . . "

Hippolyte was prey to a strange emotion. At first he felt embarrassed that his business, through Edmond's doing, should, as it were, be common knowledge even as far away as New Zealand. But now that this sin of pride had been committed, all he could do was endure the celebrity it carried with it as best he might, without seeming too puffed up about it. And such had been almost exactly Luzina's feelings. To see it proclaimed throughout the whole Empire that she had so many babies had not, at first sight, wholly pleased her; perhaps you did not win fame after the fashion you might have chosen. All the same, burdensome or agreeable, the fact remained that it was through little Edmond that they had attained it, and you could not long be cross with him over such a gift. That the letter should have been written in English, however – a tongue foreign to them, just barely understandable, far from their normal lives – was what after all gave them the greatest pride. And that honour they could relish to their hearts' content.

"So well written a letter, and not even in his own language!" said Luzina.

This child of theirs, moreover, had never done them anything but credit.

"Already in Mademoiselle Côté's time," Luzina recalled, "he answered questions well."

From a long way off she could hear: "The Little Water Hen, too, Mademoiselle?" "Of course, Edmond dear, all this, this whole country belonged to France."

Like all happy ages which ever pass too quickly, the days of the school seemed to have gone by at breakneck speed. She also heard, deep in her motherly satisfaction, a burst of laughter, perhaps a warning. "And will the little Tousignants on Water Hen island have much use for grammar and spelling?"

Well, this is what use they had for them: they wrote letters even to New Zealand; they made themselves known afar; they had friends elsewhere, in distant parts of the world; was that not an answer?

"And then, later," insisted the schoolmaster's mocking voice, "they will little by little forget what they have learned, and what good will the school have done you!"

That was the most forthright of the threats he had caused to hover over her, and it was the one she dreaded most. To forget seemed to her worse than not to have learned. To forget was to allow something that had been yours to be lost, and that was more serious than not to have tried to better yourself. Forgetting was no more nor less than thanklessness. And yet once, during an evening, they had all tried to call to mind the name of the Governor General of Canada, which they had known perfectly well.

"We did know it: we'll surely remember it," said Luzina. "Let's try hard."

But no one of them could think of the Governor's name. It seemed to be right there, in their memories; still, it amused itself by hiding, and all their efforts could not bring it to the surface. Joséphine, so loyal in remembrance, said nothing. Edmond himself declared he had forgotten. That Governor's name was, after all, not too great a loss. Hippolyte grumbled that it would not prevent their eating or sleeping in peace; but Luzina continued to rack her brain. On several occasions in full daylight they saw her sitting, her eyes vague; she was dredging for that Governor's name, which must begin with a T. One day you lost the Governor's name, said she, and the next day you lost something else. Then she began to reflect that if one of them held onto the knowledge they had acquired, all would not be lost. Her glance fell on Edmond. "Either they will little by little forget," Armand Dubreuil had said, "or they must keep on learning." Edmond was the best informed among them. Assuredly his was the right of guardianship over their knowledge. Whereupon, one eve-

ning when she was not seeking it, Luzina hit upon the
Governor's name. It was Tweedsmuir. Her fear, nonetheless, had been keen, and it remained so. Edmond was to
spare them from such alarms in the future. Meanwhile
Luzina's imagination brushed away the difficulties; she
did not fully envision the fact that to get schooling
Edmond would have to leave them, live far away. Later on
it was too late to back water. Hippolyte had agreed, thinking to please Luzina; and Luzina could not reverse herself
for fear of saddening Hippolyte. Autumn was already
close at hand. From day to day the birds were flying
higher. They were practising for their long flight. One of
these mornings, when you got up, you would be
astounded at the unwonted silence which reigned over the
deserted sedges. At dawn, when no one yet suspected
anything, the birds would have gone, and at the hour
when their going was discovered, they would already be
far away; they would have covered a good stretch of the
road to Florida where, it seemed, the sun shone bright the
year round and where there were always flowers. Even the
life of a young bird had its mysteries. They seemed to
want things that they had never known.

About the time of year when the birds emigrated from
the North, the first of the Tousignant children departed.

V

For four years now, Joséphine had been buoyed by a great
ambition: to walk about on high heels, with a light and
graceful tread like Mademoiselle's; to do her hair with tiny
curls in front like Mademoiselle; and, what was much
more difficult, to become as learned as Mademoiselle.

The very day of Mademoiselle Côté's departure,
Joséphine had followed her all the way to the mainland,
weeping large tears: "Whatever is going to become of us!"
Yet at the last minute she had pulled her book out from

under her apron and had asked: "Do at least explain this page to me before you go, Mademoiselle."

"You're now quite capable of learning by yourself," Mademoiselle Côté had encouragingly told her. "Learn a little something every day."

The whole winter through, seated in one corner of the kitchen and reading aloud, Joséphine had worked her disconsolate way to the very last page of the second reader. And she then had requested another.

She had not been overfond of the Englishwoman. The Englishwoman had not been nice, like Mademoiselle; she was not lovely-looking, like Mademoiselle. But almost equal to Joséphine's loyalty was her passion for learning. She learned from the Englishwoman because there was no one else at hand to teach her and because Mademoiselle had urged her to study hard. She knew her *Mother Goose*. She knew it all by heart, without understanding more than a half-dozen words. Yet mangling these brief tales in verse, one mistake leading on to another, without pause, full steam ahead, Joséphine was considered to have a very good knowledge of English on Little Water Hen island.

Armand Dubreuil's arrival had disappointed her. She had never thought it possible that a man could be any good at teaching. That, however, was no reason for her to abandon her tactics which consisted in learning from whoever might know a bit more than Joséphine. She took it upon herself to stalk him while he was hunting.

She would suddenly pop up in front of him, having hidden behind trees the better to keep tabs on him. "I've learned the page you told me to learn," Joséphine would announce.

She stared at him with a disapproving look in her eye; he was far from being a good schoolmaster. He took very little trouble with his explanations. You had to do it almost all by yourself. What was the difference? He was better than nothing.

"Good, very good, Joséphine. You're really a little wonder. Now go ahead and learn the next page since you're so quick at it."

"At least ask me a few questions to see if I know it," Joséphine would insist.

During the evening, her instructor still had the small girl underfoot. She would interrupt his tales of the chase; unbending, tenacious, she would force him back into his teacher's role: "What does it mean when it says the *subject* of a sentence?"

"Joséphine is a pest. In that sentence, Joséphine is the subject. She is the one who is doing the talking. She is the one who acts, and bothers me."

Though he had great faults, Armand Dubreuil made the things he taught clear. Then, too, Joséphine suspected that he, also, would be leaving soon. She buzzed around him like a bee, eager to extract all the information, all the knowledge he possessed.

Before he went, Armand Dubreuil gave them all little presents. "And you, my small nuisance, what in the world will I give you?"

Without hesitation, determined to get what she wanted, she had answered, "Your grammar." And the schoolmaster gave it to her.

What complications were to spring from this dry-as-dust gift of Joséphine's! Her head between her hands, resolved to learn, she jousted with unintelligible texts. No longer did she teach on Little Water Hen island; in vain did her pupils, Héloïse, Valmore-Gervais, and tiny Marie-Ange, stand in line and ask her to play school. Joséphine had to attend to her own advancement. One day her piping, afflicted voice drowned out all the competing sounds in the house at an instant when Luzina was busy with a score of other things.

"Mother, what is an indirect object?"

Luzina stopped stirring her broth. The void that opened in her mind dizzied her. An indirect object! Come! She must have learned that in her day! An indirect object! It was far off, much farther off than the Governor's name, and even that she had again forgotten. Probably it was lost forever. Quite the coward, Luzina told Joséphine, "Ask your father."

As for him, he did not believe he had ever known what an indirect object was. "Ask your mother."

Joséphine grew impatient. "Now, Mother! I want to know!"

Suddenly it was more than Luzina could stand. She became angry. Could she do everything! – bring up eleven unmanageable children, cook for them, mend their clothes, take care of their father who was almost as unreasonable as they and, over and above all that, still remember her grammar? God in Heaven! No one person could have done all that! What was more, she was sick and tired of this grammar business. She had heard all she wanted to hear about it.

"I'm going to burn that wretched book, that's all there is to it," Luzina decided.

Burn Joséphine's grammar! No sooner had Luzina grasped the meaning of her threat than she at once turned repentant, kindly, persuasive. What had come over her! For this long time she had lived in the midst of her children, kindly, indulgent, herself as unharassed as a child, imagining that they would become well educated, would know a great deal more than she did herself. She had never had an inkling that they would ask devastating questions, would find her ignorant.

"I'm going to show you how to sew," she offered in an excess of goodheartedness. "Get a needle and thread. It's much more useful to know how to sew than to learn grammar."

"I'm going to be a schoolteacher," said Joséphine.

"All right, then." Luzina wanted to conciliate her. "Teach your little brothers and sisters. You know a lot. Show them what you know. Play school some more."

"I'm going to be a real schoolteacher," Joséphine continued.

Then a very sly defence strategy occurred to Luzina.

"Like the poor Englishwoman, I suppose! You want to waste your life going from one wretched school to another, like our old Miss O'Rorke. There is nothing more miserable than being a schoolmistress."

"I'm not going to be a schoolmistress like Miss O'Rorke," said Joséphine with asperity. "I'm going to be a schoolteacher like Mademoiselle Côté."

"To become a schoolteacher," Luzina pointed out, "you'd have to go to a convent for years and then more years. You'd be shut in and far from home. You'd have to do what the sisters told you, all the time. And even before that, you'd have to leave all alone with old Nick Sluzick and travel alone on a big train. A little pussy like you! Do you think that makes sense?"

Quite unaware of what she was doing, Luzina had opened before Joséphine precisely the road to the great things she wanted to undertake. And indeed it was the road Joséphine would follow. She would sit up beside the mailman in the region's biggest automobile. Joséphine had seen no other. She would travel for miles and miles – a hundred miles, perhaps. She would arrive at the settlement which was ten times bigger than all the buildings at the ranch put together. She would go even farther. Wait a minute! Joséphine would go as far as Rorketon. There it was ten thousand times bigger than at Portage des Prés. And at Rorketon there were the trains. Joséphine sank deep into a kitchen chair, just as though she were installed aboard the train, and she saw all southern Manitoba coming toward her. Her braids swung to and fro with the train's jolting. Joséphine rolled along faster and faster. She blinked her eyelids as though she felt full on her face the locomotive's scorching blast. She arrived at Winnipeg. Joséphine got off her train at the capital of Manitoba. At this juncture in her trip, Joséphine reached something so colossal that she gave up any attempt at comparison with what she knew already. Quite simply, Joséphine remained suspended in the midst of the unknown, the tip of her eager tongue rubbing against her lip.

"It's well enough for the boys to go far away to school," conceded Luzina. "But a little girl does not need education as much as all that."

Joséphine cut her off short. "Mademoiselle was a girl, and she was even better educated than Monsieur Dubreuil."

"No, no, no," argued Luzina. "Monsieur Dubreuil said so himself. He has his bachelor's degree."

"You said yourself," Joséphine reminded her, "that Mademoiselle was the nicest girl in the world."

"Oh! That one!"

Luzina glanced distractedly at Mademoiselle Côté's old room. Miss O'Rorke had occupied it and turned it upside down with her mania for moving the furniture around every other day. Armand Dubreuil had transformed it into an arsenal. Finally the Capuchin Father had slept there, and yet it still was called "Mademoiselle's room." Their first teacher had left it more than four years ago, but she remained ever with them, never to be ousted, beyond criticism. She answered through the children's mouths. She won in every argument. Basically it was she who finally had pulled Edmond away and then Charles. And now it was clear that she would have Joséphine.

Luzina sat down at the big kitchen table to write to her sister Blanche, who lived at Saint Jean Baptiste, where there was a convent. She asked her whether she would be willing to take Joséphine, "a good small girl, studious, hard-working, handy, not too bothersome, stubborn as they came, but stubborn in her desire to learn. . . ." And from time to time, exasperated by the effort every letter exacted, Luzina demanded silence around her, addressing her remarks principally to Joséphine. "Obstinate girl! The sisters won't put up with the things I've put up with. . . . You'll see that it won't always be fun at the convent. . . ."

Luzina had laughed so much in her life that the wrinkles and expression of her face were fixed in a pattern of good humour. Her scoldings and complaints never seemed very serious. Just like those aged Indians whom

you can't imagine sad because their eyes, from exposure to
the sun, seem always to twinkle with engaging slyness,
poor Luzina was fated to be seriously misconstrued.
"Mama is always gay. Mama takes things well," her children would say.

It was spring, though the weather remained quite cold,
when the family ventured forth to deliver Joséphine to the
mailman. From the elevated seat of the ancient Ford,
Nick Sluzick saw a strange sight. The whole Tousignant
tribe was coming toward him in single file. The father and
one of the sons carried a box made of dark wood which,
from a distance, looked exactly like a small coffin. In their
midst walked a little girl dressed all in black. The group,
only partly visible above the rushes, moved along as
though at a burial. Hoisted to shoulder height, the wooden
box jolted through the air.

What had got into them today?

Waiting upset the old fellow's nerves. It would be at
least five minutes before the Tousignants could reach him,
and those minutes gave Sluzick ample time to ruminate
upon his life's quest for happiness.

Some fifteen years earlier he had arrived in this country
utterly without neighbours, and it had been his reasonable
belief that he would live there in peace. Nobody knew
how to read or write in those fine old days, and no one
suffered because of it. Progress, civilization, which was
what people called nuisance and botheration, had all the
same begun to overtake them, little by little, in the North.
At first people had taken it into their heads to get letters,
then mail-order catalogues. Mail-order catalogues! Just
about the silliest thing in all the world! They were cumber-
some; they filled a mail bag in no time at all, and why? I
ask you! Just to demonstrate to you that now you needed
a whole stack of things you had gotten along perfectly well
without: lamps with incandescent mantles, aluminum
saucepans, enamelled stoves. Enamelled stoves, if you

please! People had sunk to that! What was more, every spring the population increased to the point where it amounted to an epidemic. And with all their brood, the Tousignants had conceived the idea of having a schoolmistress.

His knees crossed, one leg projecting outside the car, Nick spat overboard, aiming at a dent in the mudguard.

Ugh! He should have understood that life was no longer livable in these parts the very day when he had lugged out that crazy old woman who tried to show him the road to the Little Water Hen! For five years now he had constantly been carting people back and forth. He was under a running fire. No sooner had he brought someone here in May than October was upon him and he had to carry that person all the way back. It was a fine thing to have left the heart of the Carpathian Mountains and to have crossed almost the whole of Canada only to end up with traffic as congested as it was getting to be here. Hadn't it happened, one fine day last year or the year before, that he had taken on a soldier of some kind? The chap had called himself a schoolmaster, but don't try to tell Nick Sluzick that there wasn't spy work of some sort in that business. Nick Sluzick had turned around and seen his Ford loaded to the brim with instruments of warfare. Enough to finish the old car off. It was already a wonder that the ancient vehicle ran at all. On every trip he had to crawl underneath, replace a piston, get a new wheel, unscrew the carburetor; he almost had to take it apart and put it together again for each trip. He could not be expected to lug along baggage, people, mail bags, and spies into the bargain. Nick Sluzick would sell his car that very day, while it still was in good order. Today it was in the prime of its life. Nick would get rid of it. It was a fine little car. Everything about it had been put in shape like new. It could keep on going indefinitely. So Nick would sell his old rattletrap, and then, the quicker the better, he'd clear out for Fox Island, thirty-five miles farther north. He had brought in every one of these Tousignants, one after the other, when they weren't more than ten or twelve days old, the size of rabbits. He had had a dog's time getting them there alive. They cried with cold, with hunger. Once, during the thaw, he had just avoided drowning one in a flooded stretch of road. He had almost lost one in the snow, with a March blizzard raging. It was a miracle if two or three others had not been born in his arms, on the trip out, those people always being in such a hurry. Yes, in all truth, Nick Sluzick had had troubles enough to deliver the Tousignant population alive; he had no intention now of carting them, one by one, away from their island.

Joséphine had just taken her seat between the mailman and Hippolyte, who was to see her to Rorketon. There, the conductor would be requested to take care of Joséphine and himself to put her on the Winnipeg train, he having done as much already for Edmond and Charles. Aunt Blanche was to go to the capital to meet Joséphine. Swollen with her own importance, Joséphine felt a love throb in her heart which embraced very nearly all mankind.

The mailman's nose was running copiously; his catarrh had become so bad that, summer and winter, Nick Sluzick distilled a silvery liquid which hung in threads between the hairs of his nostrils and the bristles of his moustache, crisscrossing in an intricate network and supplying him with a kind of diminutive muzzle, fine-meshed yet tough. Joséphine, however, who was off to be educated, felt a wholly fresh forbearance for the people of the region, dirty for the sole reason that they knew no better. Today something strange was gnawing at Joséphine's heart. Her great affection for all humanity was already fastening especially on the unfortunate, the ignorant whom it would later be her mission to teach. She turned toward the postman the little face of a schoolmistress who understood things.

Nick grabbed the wheel. The Ford bounced over a big mound, tumbled into a water hole, clambered up the side of the trail. Luzina had started running to catch up with it. Both arms outstretched, she stumbled against a boulder;

she could still make out the fine white piping on Joséphine's black dress. She stopped. Her eyes grew wide. Luzina suddenly saw much more than a detail of her daughter's clothing. For a long time it had been she alone who had travelled. Almost every year she had departed and hurried about her business in order to come home with one more child against a wilderness to be peopled. Now she remained behind, and it was the children who were leaving. After a fashion, Luzina was seeing life. And she could not believe what her stout heart told her: already life, to which she had given so abundantly, little by little was leaving her behind.

XI

She could no longer keep up the pace. She had more children, but at far greater intervals, and soon it seemed that that was finished. The children, however, continued to go their ways. After Joséphine, André-Aimable and Roberta-Louise. Where had the latter picked up her compelling desire to become a nurse? The only explanation was that one communicated to the next the ancient illness with which Mademoiselle Côté had infected the house. Hardly had Joséphine left when Héloïse had set herself up as schoolteacher for the Little Water Hen. She taught that there were nine provinces, that the world was big, ten thousand times as big as Portage des Prés. How true that was, alas! Edmond and Charles were at school at the academy in Saint Boniface; one of Hippolyte's uncles, a parish priest, was paying their board and lodging. Edmond was studying literature; Charles had progressed as far as rhetoric; in her letters Joséphine spoke of compound addition and of botany. She had been given a medal by Bishop Yelle, Bishop Beliveau's coadjutor.

There had been a time when Luzina could direct her children's studies: *a, e, i, o, u*; another period when she succeeded more or less in keeping up with them. Evenings, the kitchen turned into a study hall. There the pupils spread out their manuals and notebooks. "Mama, the ink bottle." Luzina snuffed the lamp; you must take good care of your eyes if you wanted to do your lessons properly. She fetched her own homework, the family mending. If she had to get up to find thread or another needle, she did it quietly, on tiptoe. She would sit down again at education's edge. And she would grasp her small share of it. While she patched the seat of a pair of trousers, she would pick up a requirement of grammar, a snatch of history. Frontenac informed the commander of the British fleet: "I shall answer you with the mouths of my cannon!"

From her corner, Luzina spoke her approval: "Well answered." Her needle flew. In the length of time it took to repair Edmond's pants, the English were repulsed. How pleased she was at the ill-tempered old Governor in those days gone by! Having never seen a fleet or a cannon, Luzina had no muddled images in her pleasant reconstruction of history. After all, it was not so much the victory of one side or the defeat of the other that interested her, but rather the fact of learning. She would store a date away, in the same fashion as she would set aside a spool of thread or a scrap of cloth, saying to herself, "I must remember that." And she had done it to such good purpose that from time to time she could produce some bit of information precisely when it was of use. Mademoiselle Côté herself had been taken aback by this. "Do you realize, Madame Tousignant, that you have a great deal of natural ability?" For having said this alone, Luzina could have thrown her arms around the teacher's neck. Luzina was not an unhappy woman; she did not believe she had any reason to complain. Her life seemed to her as good as she deserved; and yet there were times when she had felt a brief twinge in her heart, that sadness at not being wholly understood which is common to all who dwell upon this earth. So it was, in all truth, the keen joy of having had her shy taste for learning discovered and not held up to ridicule – it was that joy which the teacher's kindly words had made sparkle in Luzina's eyes, suddenly alight with gratitude. After the evening's lessons, she went to bed almost as overexcited as the children; she repeated to herself what she had heard; her housewife's tasks complicated her life as a pupil; her two sets of cares became intertwined. She began to progress more slowly. And then, abruptly, she was left behind. Never again would she be able to catch up with the children. Syntax, Latin, Greek! The Bishop's medal!

Occasionally Luzina would still enter the small schoolhouse. The birches had grown and cast a great deal of shadow over the windows which Hippolyte had wanted opening on as much light as possible. Within the tiny room the light was now green and sad. In order to mount the platform, Luzina had to clamber over lengths of stovepipe, coils of rope, and she had to push aside a grindstone. The school smelt of mould, the smell of old, damp paper. Luzina pulled the string of one of the large maps sent long ago by the government. Manitoba hung in front of her, almost as big as the wall. Here and there the sturdy paper had come somewhat loose from its muslin backing; there were places where Manitoba was swollen in blisters, like those maps on which mountain chains are shown in relief. Here, however, it was the even plain that rose, sank back, split open. An underwater glow played over the old map, wrinkled as it was and spotted with green. You might have imagined that it sought to show Luzina a world which everywhere had reasons for growing sorrowful. At the very bottom of the map Luzina saw an area fairly black with the names of rivers, villages, and towns. That was the South. Almost every village had its geographical rights in the South. Luzina's finger went exploring along the lines of longitude and latitude. Lovingly she would now and then seek to smooth out the map's wrinkles. At last she would discover Otterburne, the precise spot where André-Aimable was studying apiculture with the Viatorians. Her finger moved along farther. Here, at Saint Jean Baptiste, she located young Héloïse, whom Aunt Blanche had sent for the moment Joséphine had made sufficient progress. Luzina moved upward to find Roberta-Louise at the Dauphin hospital. The old map seemed to her almost a friend – and likewise a thief. It oozed moisture. As she stroked it lightly and warmed it with her hand, Luzina extracted from it little drops of humidity, thin, cold, which under her finger gave her a strange impression of tears. Then Manitoba seemed to her to grow bored. So vast, so little bestrewn with names, almost entirely given over to those wide, naked stretches which represented lakes and uninhabited space! Emptier and emptier, bare paper without a printed word, the farther you went into the North. It seemed that all the place names had clustered together on this map as though to warm each other, that they had all crowded together in the same corner of the South. There they even had to be abbreviated, so small was the available space, but up above they stretched out at their ease, with room to spare. Mademoiselle Côté had taught that three-quarters of Manitoba's population all dwelt within this little portion of the map that Luzina could cover with her two hands. That left very few people for the North! So vacant in that portion, the old map seemed to want to take vengeance on Luzina. In large letters it bore the name Water Hen River. It was silent, however, regarding the existence of the island in the Little Water Hen.

Luzina sat down briefly at the schoolmistress's desk, high up on the platform. Joséphine must be a big girl by now. Her Aunt Blanche wrote that she had won another prize. In a competition sponsored by the Manitoba Association of French Canadians, she had been given the award for French established by the Manitoba Federation of French Canadian Ladies. "I wish you could have seen her," wrote her aunt, "in the white dress I made her for the prize-day ceremonies at the convent." Some day soon Luzina would receive a small photo ordered from Winnipeg as well as one of Héloïse, and she would see that the younger girl was also looking well. Edmond had landed an "accessit" in English. He, likewise, had always had an aptitude for English. *Accessit!* In one of the teacher's desk drawers there was still a small dictionary. To be certain she could lay hands on it when she needed it, Luzina had insisted that it was better to keep it in its proper place, which was Mademoiselle Côté's drawer. She looked *accessit* up. "Honour awarded in schools or in academies to those who have come closest to winning a prize. . . . " So! It was not the prize itself, but only an approach to it! Luzina had thought that it was more than that. Perhaps Edmond had had the ground pushed out from under his feet by some teacher's pet. Poor Miss O'Rorke! Where was she now? Luzina had heard from her once. Miss O'Rorke had written that she felt old and that she was thinking of retiring at last and going back to her beloved Ontario and civilization. She inquired after Edmond. She would have been pleased to have learned that he had won an accessit in English. Poor Englishwoman! With the passage of time, Luzina had made her a real friend of her heart, the only woman in the world perhaps fully to understand solitude. Suddenly she thought she heard a rustling sound, as though someone were turning a book's pages. She glanced towards a dark corner of the schoolroom. It was only some field mice nuzzling a discarded copy book. For five years now Blanche had been saying that she would some day come to see this famous Water Hen country and that she would bring the girls with her. Never having had any daughters, Blanche claimed that the Good Lord Himself had sent Joséphine and later Héloïse to be the consolation and pride of her life. As for Hippolyte's uncle, the parish priest, he talked about his nephews as though he had somehow succeeded, by himself alone, in bringing them into the world. Luzina would love to have seen him, now and again, sitting with his belly all swollen alongside the postman in a blizzard; and it was "Smack your horse, my old Nick Sluzick, if you want me to get there in time . . . and you, too, Ivan Bratislovski, smack your horse!"

She saw herself again, jolting over the hardened crust along the wretched trail. Would she arrive in time? Would she not arrive at all? She did take precautions; she tried to depart at least a week early. After all, she could not leave the family to its own devices indefinitely. She changed relays hurriedly. Sometimes the joltings and anxieties of the trip hastened nature's processes. She was not yet at ease even when at last she clambered aboard the train. This was not the moment for relaxing. She was on the verge of begging the engineer to put on speed. The old peg-legged conductor knew her; every five minutes he would come and ask her whether she felt all right. The wheels turned, the locomotive whistled. Before coming into the world, Luzina's children knew every kind of terror, every means of transportation and, finally, this last stretch by train which, with its whistle blasts and the hammering of wheels on rails, seemed especially to stir them up. Almost always Luzina reached the Sainte Rose du Lac hospital at the last possible moment. No sooner had she entered its front door than old Dr Magnan arrived on her heels, out of breath. He would scold her: "For Heaven's sake, have you set out to populate the Little Water Hen all by yourself! . . . "

Luzina returned to the present. She found herself sitting alone in the tiny schoolroom; she smiled for an instant at the recollection of her ancient prowess. Then at once she rejoiced to think that some few of her children had escaped from the difficulties she had known.

Her resentment against Hippolyte's uncle turned into gratitude. Even he himself could not know from what a wilderness he had extricated them. Thinly peopled as it was, the Little Water Hen country had nevertheless found means to empty itself.

Luzina's nearest neighbours, halfbreeds named Mackenzie, who for six months had been living on the mainland two miles from the ranch, at about the spot where the postman left the mail, had just decamped.

Their departure, moreover, had dealt the final blow to

Luzina's hope of some day seeing her little school reopen. In her negotiations with the government, she now dealt with a Mr Stewart J. Acheson. Whatever had happened to that good Mr Evans? Luzina missed him; his successor was far less accommodating. He required at least seven pupils of enrollment age, and that meant between six and fourteen, with no leeway at all. Of small Tousignants within those age brackets there remained only four at home. But the Mackenzies had six children. They were almost wholly wild, half-naked, grimy, speaking the Lord knew what language – a little English, a smattering of French, and probably some Saultais mingled perhaps with a few words of Cree. No matter! Luzina had cast a greedy eye in their direction. She had paid the Mackenzies a visit. A small log hut, dirty, smoky, furnished with straw mattresses lying directly on the floor. The family's Indian blood was particularly apparent in the mother. Shifty eyes, hypocritical, timorous. Luzina had been friendly, enthusiastic. She had brought with her fresh butter and pembina jam the better to persuade the halfbreeds of the advantages of education. "If we write the government – both families together – we can force their hand; we should be sure of getting a schoolmistress." Wasted effort. The halfbreeds regarded school as something like prison, a dungeon complete with bars. Luzina had then made the blunder of introducing the law into her pleasant descriptions of education. All children between six and fourteen were supposed to go to school. That was the law, and a serious business. You made yourself subject to fines and other penalties if you evaded the law. The government had inspectors who came to ferret out recalcitrant children in their own homes. The government had a long arm.

Perhaps she thus succeeded in making the Mackenzies clear out sooner than they would have in their normal routine of sudden moves. Placed where game most abounded within an area of forty miles, they possessed three other cabins similar to that where they occasionally sojourned along Nick Sluzick's route. Then, too, it was a simple matter for them to break camp. Like the Indians, they owned almost nothing, and that little – a stove and some pots – they gladly left behind them so that they might the more freely leave.

XII

The winters seemed to become harsher and harsher along the Little Water Hen. That year, before the end of October snow covered the entire island. Everywhere stiff whiteness. The tufts of reeds, rounded under their mantles of snow, resembled frozen sheep; and thus the winter landscape in some fashion reminded you of summer. The wind, however, was terrifically violent. In its sweep across so many an icy plain, so many motionless rivers, lakes frozen solid – space held captive and affording it no other obstacle than spindly sedge grasses – the wind acquired an insane velocity. The Tousignant dwelling, with its thick walls, its squat length, its small windows near the ground, was the first house the northwest gale encountered on its journey from the North Pole. The gale belaboured it furiously as though there were some absolute need to make an example of this spearhead of man's encroachment which, were the wind to leave it alone, would tomorrow find reinforcement, sturdier means of resistance.

Only twice a day did they dare open the door and face the elements. Hippolyte, heavy and bulging in his sheepskin, lantern in hand even at midday, set out for the sheepfold. It was not far off, about a hundred feet, but more than once it happened that Hippolyte could reach it only on snowshoes, holding his hurricane lantern in front of him like a man trying to find the road at night in some strange country. The wind never ceased. No sooner had they succeeded in beating a path from the house to the outbuildings than the fresh snow blotted the path out. One blizzard would blow itself to an end, only to be followed by another blast out of the North. Here were most powerful enemies arrayed against the island's only living beings: a few hundred sheep, squeezed into a confused, astonished mass, almost invisible in the twilight of their shelter, a few domestic animals, and in the house five human beings in all. Of Luzina's large family there remained to help the father only Pierre and Norbert; for Luzina herself there was Claire-Armelle, the surprise package.

She had had this surprise at the age of forty-six. One evening, four years earlier, Luzina had gone to find Hippolyte at the sheep pen. She had sat down on one of the bars of the enclosure's fence as she used to in the old days when she was still a young woman and when, not having enough children to keep her busy, she would get bored in the house and, in the middle of the working day, go out to chat with Hippolyte. Seeing her perched upon the fence, he had known at once that she had news. And she, for the first time in years, had recaptured her fine, open laugh, rich and a trifle dovelike.

"We couldn't have hit it worse if we'd tried for a hundred years," said Luzina. "This time, my man, your wife's holiday comes plumb in the middle of February!"

And, in very fact, the "surprise" and her mother had travelled in weather seldom experienced even in Manitoba's frozen wasteland. Snow, wind, bad roads, excessive cold – all had joined forces against the two voyagers. Perhaps this was why Luzina so greatly cherished her surprise. Together they had outfaced more misery than many a human being encounters throughout his whole lifetime. Perhaps it was even more because Luzina firmly believed that no power in the world could separate her from her little Claire-Armelle.

The winter continued its rigours. In December the snow, almost daily shovelled to either side of the doorway, made a sort of tunnel at the end of which for a brief moment you could see the sun's red face; whereupon the light faded away.

Then it was that Luzina conceived the idea of having Joséphine's former tiny school desk brought into the house and placed near the stove. The school was buried in snow up to the tops of its three small windows; its door was completely covered. Even when it had been freed of its encumbering snow, it refused to open. It had sagged of its own weight, and water had collected on its surface and frozen it solid to the jamb. They had to force it with a pickaxe and pour boiling water into its joints. Hippolyte had grumbled that if Luzina was so keen about having Joséphine's desk, she should have told him so before winter. One day, all the same, he came in carrying the rough little piece of furniture in his arms; it was damp from its long stay in the schoolhouse, and here and there it was powdered with snow.

Joséphine's tiny desk! Despite her obstinacy in asking for it during the last several weeks, Luzina would not have believed how eager she was to see it again. In her mind's eye the house was – for an instant – full of children, as in days gone by, each in his corner, studying his lessons out loud. Joséphine was the shrillest of all – yet she herself in those days had not adequately understood her little girl's ambition and had sometimes teased her for wanting to become as learned as Mademoiselle. She rushed to the sideboard to find Joséphine's most recent letter. It was Joséphine's first year as a teacher. She had written: "Dear Mama, when I went into my classroom this morning and I saw the children's faces turn toward me, I certainly thought of you. This happiness I in large part owe, dear Mama, to your spirit of sacrifice, to your devotion. . . . "

During her lifetime Luzina had read as many novels as she had been able to lay her hands on. Almost all of them had made her cry, were their endings sad or happy. It was simply that stories' endings, in themselves, induced in her regret beyond consoling. The lovelier the tale had been, the more did she grieve to see it end. Yet in what novel issuing from an author's pen had she beheld a better-managed ending, one more satisfying than that which crowned her own life – and one to make her weep more tears! "Deep thanks from the bottom of my heart . . .

your devotion ... your self-sacrifice ... you it was who gave us a taste for learning. ... " Joséphine expressed herself as well as they do in books. Her even, careful handwriting lent weight, as Luzina saw it, to sentiments already so well put. The summit of all difficult things for her consisted in apt words written in a steady hand with letters clear and well shaped. Respectfully she recognized this in the most unfamiliar expressions Joséphine used: the ideal, vocation, fulfilment of personality. She lingered over it also in Edmond's letters, but here it was less striking; Edmond did not have a fine handwriting. To think, though, that he was finishing his medical studies at Laval University, in that same city of Quebec from whence Mademoiselle Côté's old Governor had replied with the mouths of his cannon! Could they even have suspected, in the days when they heard about Frontenac at the Water Hen, that Edmond would one day with his own eyes see the citadel of French resistance! And thus Luzina glimpsed, at times, her own strange greatness through this ultimate distance separating her from her children.

Nevertheless, a little further on in Joséphine's letter she wrinkled her forehead: "Now that I'm earning something," Joséphine wrote, "I shall assume responsibility for the education of one of the children. It's certainly my turn. You realize that we can't neglect little Claire-Armelle. So I hope that within a few years you'll be able to send her to me. ... "

No, certainly not! The priest uncle had had three children. Aunt Blanche three more. Dr Pambrun of Saint Boniface had had Edmond, whom he was helping in his studies. The South had attracted others who had been keen to live nearer their fellows. Some few were not very far away, true enough, married and settled at Rorketon and Sainte Rose du Lac. All of them, what was more, were eager to have Luzina and Hippolyte near them. "Why continue to live on the Water Hen?" they asked. Luzina had made a grand tour to see them all again. But at Winnipeg she had felt lost. It was not at all the city she remembered from the days of her honeymoon. The Parliament building had seemed fearful to her, icy, and the buffaloes even heavier than she recalled them. Moreover, she could never again have all her children around her. When she would be in the South, she would think of those who were at Rorketon and on the ranch; at Rorketon she missed those at Saint Jean Baptiste; from Saint Jean Baptiste her thoughts would flit to Dauphin; and so it went. It was during her visit in civilized parts, likewise, that she best heard the plaintive, monotonous call, the persistent call, of the little water hens. She had come back the quickest way she knew with her small Claire-Armelle, who had accompanied her on the great tour.

This one the good Lord had given her to be the staff of her old age.

Yet the days were long. Writing to every corner of the land did not wholly use up the winter hours. The snow fell against the panes in moist flakes which were kept from sliding down by the black wooden mullions; little by little these supports piled the snow up until it almost blocked each pane. You could look outdoors through a narrow strip of glass just the width of the eye peering through it. The metal doorknob was covered with rime and colder to the touch than an icicle.

To while away the time, Luzina one day took the small "surprise" by the hand and led her to Joséphine's writing desk. Still heavy and plump, Luzina could just squeeze onto one edge of the desk. The wind was howling. Close beside her tiny daughter, Luzina began showing her her letters. "That's *A*," said Luzina. "*A* like your brother Aimable. *A* like little Armelle."

In a short time, in two or three years perhaps, the pupil had a better hand than her teacher. At least Luzina thought so. The content of the letters, all the things she must not forget to remind them about – health, good conduct, generosity of heart – remained Luzina's province. But for that which would be visible to the mails, to the postman, to that intermediary between herself and her children's pride, which must not be wounded, Luzina turned to Claire-Armelle.

From then on the letters which left the Little Water Hen were written along the usual slope, but the envelope bore another calligraphy. It was a handwriting extremely careful, childishly accurate. When they examined the envelopes closely, Edmond and Joséphine could make out the not wholly erased pencil lines which Luzina had drawn to help the small girl write straight.

And Luzina's educated children momentarily felt their hearts contract, as though their childhood back there, on the island in the Little Water Hen, had reproached them for their high estate.

The Capuchin From Toutes Aides

MANITOBA'S lakes are grouped in such fashion as to form an almost complete barrier for the country they enclose: very large bodies of water like Lake Winnipeg and Lake Manitoba; others which would seem large indeed when not compared to these two, such as Lake Winnipegosis and Lake Dauphin; and almost all are joined together on the map's emptiness by blue networks representing unknown rivers. But of names of towns, villages, inhabited places along their banks – almost nothing. Here is one of the world's least peopled regions, a sad, lost land, where nonetheless you encounter representatives of almost every race on earth – as many nationalities among these lakes as there are exiles. When he arrived there, Father Joseph-Marie knew nearly a score of languages.

He spoke English, French, German, Italian, a little Latvian; his father Belgian and his mother Russian, by a complex set of circumstances he had been born in Riga, and there he had spent a part of his childhood. He also spoke the Walloon dialect, Russian, and Dutch with a Flemish accent. In the plains of the South where, before coming to Toutes Aides, he had for a time ministered to a small Manitoban parish in which there lived two Magyar families, he had from them learned a little Hungarian. He knew a few words of Slovak. All that had not sufficed for hearing the sins of his two or three hundred parishioners, scattered over an area of about a hundred square miles.

He had had to learn the speech peculiar to the Polish Galicians, the tongue of the Icelandic fishermen living on the western shore of Lake Winnipegosis, the Polish of the Piriouk family and of others dwelling in Rorketon, and finally the Ruthenian variants of Ukrainian. In those days, always eager to converse with the people he met, were they his parishioners or not, Father Joseph-Marie, when he went on a trip, used to stick into a pocket of his habit a small lexicon of Saultais words, compiled by one of his Oblate friends.

This time, as he left the tiny monastery at Toutes Aides, the Capuchin was prepared for a tour of six or seven weeks. He was happy. Community life weighed on him, even here, in a house reduced to three monks and their lay brother.

He greeted Father Theodulus, who attended to the Toutes Aides parish. Each to his own taste. To have an imitation-brick church, a nave with semicircular arches and columns of fake marble, its ceiling sprinkled with blue stars pasted on Donaconna board, did not seem the greatest of all joys to Father Joseph-Marie. He did not laugh at it; he did not even deny that paper stars on a background of wood-pulp wallboard might on occasion raise souls toward heaven; not much was needed to transport the heart. But such were not achievements for which he felt he had any talent.

He also said good-bye to Brother Como, who was peeling vegetables, and to Father Chrysogonus, a great scholar and man of letters, who in a highly specialized periodical resolved subtle points of dogma. Let each labour in his own vineyard; then the world wagged well. Cheerful, striding along, smiling with his eye at the freshness of the summer morning, Father Joseph-Marie set forth.

The village of Toutes Aides lay a trifle helter-skelter on the shores of a deep bay at the tip of Lake Manitoba. It was situated in a region somewhat more rolling than elsewhere in this almost always flat country; it included a number of low places invaded by aquatic grasses, stretches of stagnant water, but also slight elevations not unkindly to agriculture. You could see on the slopes of these low hills strips of rye and fields of potatoes. In comparison with other villages on the lakes, Toutes Aides was a very advanced parish, a remarkable triumph over the bush, the muddy water, and the boulders. Father Joseph-Marie, who had traversed it after a dozen long paces, found the village rather pleasing today. He had not yet become aware that he felt friendly to Toutes Aides especially at the moment when he was leaving it.

He walked fast, his feet spread far apart as though he were wearing snowshoes. At the foot of the gentle slope which lay before the village stood the store and dwelling of old man Minard, and here the priest usually found a lift. His body, thrust forward, was kept in equilibrium by the swinging of his right arm, which put one in mind of the movement of a well-sweep. His cap furnished his skull inadequate protection against the sun – a skull far balder than the tonsure alone would have made it; at his heels his habit dragged in the dust and pebbles. His beard projected a bit in front of him, a long, thin beard, reddish like his robes, and divided into two extended strands which the wind was now stretching and lifting in the air. Upon everything, upon the dirt road he was following, upon the lake, upon the relentless sky, upon the wild roses that spread at his feet, the Capuchin fixed the lively, friendly, jovial glance of his pale blue eyes. Father-Marie had not yet observed that he above all felt the surge and joy of love of man and God when, like the Saviour Himself, he took to the road.

II

His own great achievement, his most extraordinary achievement, was at Rorketon. He did not yet view it as complete, as a featherbed on which he might henceforward take his ease. One or two small items were lacking to the ultimate embellishment and perfection of his missions. And it was precisely about these two or three minor lacunae that he was reflecting that morning as he sat on the seat of the cattle truck alongside the trader Isaac Boussorvski, who bought animals along the way with the intent of shipping them from Rorketon to Winnipeg by rail.

Upon leaving Toutes Aides, he had also left Lake Manitoba behind, and the Capuchin would see no more wide stretches of water until long after he had quit Rorketon, when he would strike the tail of Lake Winnipegosis. He settled back, pleased for the time being with the change of scenery on that stage of his journey which he called his dry trek, although there was no lack of water in the shape of small pools, swamps, and sink holes. The farmhouses were still low-lying, widely separated; the farms were small in area, but the hay was coming nicely; from time to time you could see fine herds. In short, this region seemed astoundingly rich and fertile after the sandy lake shores, constantly exposed to wind, and it became more so the nearer you got to Rorketon, which after its fashion served as a minor agricultural capital.

Along the road, Isaac Boussorvski had done satisfactory business. Behind the truck's front seat half a dozen calves bewilderedly huddled together. Isaac was driving at a good pace. Several times had the Capuchin travelled in this way, either with some competitor of Isaac's or with a government agricultural agent or with the Mounted Police, as the opportunity at hand might correspond with his personal requirements. But he had never yet taken the trip with Isaac. Isaac was reputed to have a fine nest egg, not in the Rorketon bank, where it would have countered his attempts to pass for a poor man, but at Sainte Rose du Lac. Moreover, with his very own eyes the Capuchin had just seen him strike three advantageous bargains, not inordinately profitable, however, and he was happy for everyone concerned – for the farmers who had received their reasonable share, for Isaac who all the same would do even better. His hands tucked in his sleeves, he was mak-

ing up his mind to talk about the things he needed at
Rorketon before he would be fully content. It seemed to
him that Saint Joseph, who was his guide in such situa-
tions, had already nudged his elbow and had whispered to
him this advice: "Isaac is richer than most people think;
you must ask him for a small contribution for the Rorketon chapel." Reasonably enough, nonetheless, the Capuchin objected to Saint Joseph that, Isaac not even having
been baptized, it was rather indelicate to have him pay for
the objects of a cult he did not approve. Which led him to
the reflection that in money matters the faithful were not
necessarily the most favoured. As Saint Joseph remained
silent on this point, the Capuchin began talking again, but
on a subject far removed from that of any small contribution. His companion was one of those short, round Jews,
fat and extremely voluble, who talk as much with the
hands as with the mouth and tell funny stories about
themselves; the Capuchin could not reconcile these pleasant traits with a basic rapacity or a pinchpenny attitude.
Isaac could not be as rich as he was said to be. Then, too,
it was more than he could manage: whenever the Capuchin wanted to complain, he succeeded only in making
the most of everything he possessed. When he resumed
the conversation, you might have thought that he was the
wealthier of the two. According to him, he had at Rorketon a pleasant chapel, built of sound planks, weathertight
and without a leak anywhere. About the cabin alongside
it, which served him as presbytery, he could not say as
much. Yet whenever the weather was too bad, his neighbour, good Mrs Macfarlane, placed a very clean, warm
little room at his disposal. There were so many kind people on this earth; you were constantly meeting them. He
didn't have to worry about his food; his neighbours gave
him bread, fish, and sometimes even sweets, little delica-
cies for which he had lost all taste and which he ate only in
order not to wound those who offered them to him. Oh,
yes! The world was a pleasant place of sojourn! And to
think that it would be better yet in Heaven! Thus did the

Capuchin ramble on, in Polish, the cattle merchant's mother tongue.

Hearing Polish carried Isaac back to the wretchedness of his youth. He appraised the road he had covered since: "Not bad, not at all bad, Isaac Boussorvski!" As had happened with many another, he wondered how the Capuchin could have learned so many languages. Had he lived the life of a man rich and privileged, and was that the explanation of his great learning? To look at him, you would not think so. Where, then, had he garnered so much knowledge? There was not a subject on which you could catch him wholly ignorant, and no way of knowing how he had learned it all. Father Joseph-Marie was not a person to whom you put questions. You did not understand why. He himself asked as many questions as he liked, and in the end he knew everything, with his little eyes on the lookout for news, his thick eyebrows knotted with interest, his way of injecting himself into the anecdote to which he was listening, his face alight as though nothing could please him more than the lives of others. Even on such occasions you did not feel you had the right to inquire, for instance, "And you, yourself, Father Joseph-Marie, where do you come from? Who are you?" Perhaps because of his utter simplicity. Everything that was odd in itself seemed natural in the Capuchin, even the fact that he talked exactly like a Jew from Lwow. Meanwhile they were drawing close to Rorketon, and the Capuchin had not yet found a way to let it be known that his chapel still lacked a statue of Saint Joseph.

Saint Joseph was frankly his favourite saint. He would say that Saint Joseph was not sufficiently appreciated. Everything about the life of Jesus' foster-father was made in order to please him: his most chaste function as guardian and protector; and then, naturally, his travels – the trip to Bethlehem for the census, the flight into Egypt and, later, the three days spent in searching for the Child. On the flight into Egypt especially Father Joseph-Marie meditated for long hours; he asked himself how the Saint had gone about getting the Child milk, for after all the Boy was then too young to live on figs and dates.

The time was very brief, now, for launching the subject properly to Isaac. To start at the beginning and explain how Isaac, had he lived in ancient Judea, might very easily have met the carpenter Joseph – alas! the minutes remaining to him were too few. He had lost a great deal of time along the way in admiring the landscape, in asking the names of the few farmers he did not yet know or simply in savouring this truck ride, so comfortable and quick compared to the horse-drawn journeys of other days.

"In my time I have witnessed a great deal of progress in this country," he remarked, raising his voice very high to make it carry above the grinding of the planks in the truck's body, each striving to rattle harder than its neighbour, and exactly at the moment when a bump bounced him off the seat. "It's all very well to talk against progress," he continued. "It's all the same pleasanter to ride in a fine big vehicle like yours, Isaac, than in a bullock cart!"

"It's only an old truck on the verge of giving up the ghost, and I paid far too much for it anyway," Isaac complained, by way of precaution.

Yet if there was anyone who felt at ease at that moment it was Isaac. He liked to have a companion on the villainous road between Toutes Aides and Rorketon, in case he had a blowout, and even if that were not to happen, for the sake of not being left to his own devices for, at times a bit morbid, Isaac had a more sorrowful outlook on things when he travelled alone. Nothing boosted his morale as much as having with him, from the start, some pitiable traveller or, better yet, a poor wretch he saw trudging along the road. Faded clothes, rags, worn-out shoes with holes in them, a downcast air – here were details which for him took the place of a lesson in morals. "That is what you might have been, my lad," said Isaac to himself, "had you not scraped and saved. Yes, indeed, take a good look at what you would have been." Generosity on this earth, however, is almost always accompanied by grave disadvantages. Many of the tramps Isaac picked up along the road had been emboldened by his kindness to ask him for the price of a meal, a glass of beer, or even a room to sleep in at Rorketon. Hence Isaac had made very few trips without a worry in his mind. And how agreeable it was at last to meet a man who needed absolutely nothing and spent the whole time saying so! Yet was this completely sincere? This disposition to ask for nothing was one of the rarest things in the world. It was hard to reconcile with the monastery at Toutes Aides, the church that mimicked brick and all those splendours which were the talk of the countryside. How did the monks get so much if they asked nothing? Isaac wanted to be confirmed in his relief.

"You have a fine little chapel, a presbytery to your taste, and even a small stove to do your cooking? You have everything you need?"

"Yes," agreed the Capuchin, a little troubled at heart that feelings of delicacy made him overlook such leading questions. "Did I also tell you, Isaac, about my harmonium? I wonder at the way God has heaped my measure!"

"Perhaps you've had some small hand in it," said Isaac thoughtfully.

He halted the truck on the outskirts of the village, in front of the plank enclosure alongside the railway spur from which cattle cars were loaded. The Capuchin drew up his skirts, with the idea of climbing down and helping the trader.

"Do wait a moment," Isaac requested him.

He felt a queer obligation. Men who asked for nothing did not swarm over this world; perhaps this was the only one alive. Was it not fitting to reward him well in order the better to teach the others a lesson? Isaac thrust his hand into his pocket. He hoped he could extract from the wad of money stuffed there a one-dollar bill. That would be enough; indeed, it would be handsome. He fumbled for a while and at last extracted a banknote. Unfortunately it was for two dollars. The Capuchin, however, had already seen it; his eyes shone. To replace the two dollars with one would be cruel. Isaac had only to put himself in the Capuchin's place to realize how cruel. He had no desire to see abate that lively gleam in his companion's eyes. That would have been like whittling away his satisfaction at his own kindness, an extravagant kindness, to be sure, but one that he cherished now that he recognized it. "What's more, the man has asked me for nothing," Isaac recalled. "That's altogether extraordinary; I must make an example out of him." Then too, had he not let luck guide his hand? Luck had chosen the two-dollar bill for the Capuchin's use. All in all, thought Isaac, a great benefaction on occasion was good policy. It sheltered the benefactor for life against further importunities.

As he walked away, having pocketed the gift and thanked Isaac, the Capuchin's conclusion was wholly different. "Today Isaac gives me two dollars. The habit of giving comes from giving. Another opportunity will perhaps arise. The next time the Lord will guide Isaac's hand to the bottom of his pocket, toward a five-dollar bill. And in the end I'll surely buy a statue of Saint Joseph."

And, when you came to think of it, the statue belonged to Saint Joseph by right. For who, were it not Saint Joseph himself, could have succeeded in extracting for himself a gift of two dollars toward his own statue from a trader who had journeyed from Poland in a cattle ship in order to buy and sell animals in Manitoba! At a good pace the Capuchin reached the centre of the village. He laughed quietly in his heart at the astonishing way in which Heaven knows how to turn, without their suspecting it, men's lives to good account.

III

On Saturday nights at Rorketon, the villagers throng the principal street, busy at making bargains and staring into shop windows, and the wooden sidewalks resound briskly with the men's heavy boots and the "belles' " pointed heels. Custom in these new villages insists that everybody, even those with nothing to do, shall on Saturday nights walk up and down Main Street. It is an attraction equivalent to the arrival of the train, and who could have no feeling for it after an all too quiet week! The women even less than the men. The idea is to stroll to the end of the sidewalk, come back the way you have gone, and then repeat the process for hour after hour. This coming and going of faces – repeating themselves fairly often, for the sidewalk is not very long – succeeds at first glance in making a hundred, perhaps two hundred, people look like a considerable crowd. That is one of the charming illusions characteristic of the "frontier" villages which have sprung up at a rail head, perched between the wilderness and communication with the world outside. But at Rorketon, in addition to being numerous, the crowd is most varied. You would have to be in Winnipeg itself, in the neighbourhood of the Royal Alexandra Hotel and the Canadian Pacific station, in the old immigrants' quarter, to see in so short a time so many dissimilar types. There are Slav women with immaculate white kerchiefs knotted under their chins; peasants with long drooping moustaches, probably Russians; emigrants from Central Europe still wearing uncreased hats of soft felt, straight as stovepipes. The farmers of the neighbourhood buy at Sam Boudry's General Store; in one corner of that store a small group chats in one tongue; by the doorway another group talks a language wholly different. Standing in front of the gas pump while they have the garage man repair their ancient car, four or five individuals spit on the ground and talk animatedly, punctuating each phrase with *toc*, *toc*; they must be Ukrainians from the Ukraine itself or from Roumania. Others are still drifting in along the rutted roads, bordered with sweetbrier. They wear broad hats of yellow straw and sit stiffly on the seats of a buckboard, one holding a small green branch in his hand to serve as whip, and sometimes beside the revolving wheel trots a small farm dog which has come to sniff the village's social life.

The whole procession – buggies, dogs, women, farmers, the village belles fresh from their curling irons and redolent of Florida Water, the Protestant minister, drunks, the Capuchin priest – ends up at about the same spot, either in front of the post office or immediately next to it, in front of the General Store. Tied nose to nose to the hitching posts, the horses fidget and swish the flies with their tails.

Within the space of five minutes the Capuchin, headed for his chapel, had time to overhear a tag end of a Lithuanian conversation and pick up a good evening murmured in Finnish. Through the open doors of the Chinese restaurant he overheard quarrelling on the ancient Ukrainian theme of the hereditary hetman. He thought he spotted, from her embroidered blouse, an immigrant woman who must be from Bessarabia. Someone saluted him in the singing, rolling French of the halfbreeds, "Evening, Father." In the midst of all these greetings, he became aware of a language especially suited to stir his heart; quickly he turned about to see who it was who had spoken Flemish. He was at his ease as he stepped through this tiny Babel. That the ten or a dozen nationalities represented in Rorketon could get along so well together, gossip, laugh, and sing together, was that not ultimate, irrefutable proof that mankind is made for peace! The sounds of lively arguments reached him as he passed – from the rear of the billiard parlour, from the bar, and even from the theatre where, that evening, a dance and festival were being held. But join together a hundred people of the same race, speaking the same language, all baptized, and would you for those reasons have perfect understanding? The Capuchin had an air of asking each person he met, one after the other, at random, his naïve question, and of answering it himself by a slight nod of the head, affirmative and kindly, for he greeted people to the right, to the left, on the other side of the street, and sometimes, with a quick twist of his body, behind him. On the whole, was it not in a small crowd of well-mixed races, such as he then saw before him, that stood revealed, in its most simple natural fulfilment, the precept "Love one another!"

Oh, those evenings when he arrived at Rorketon! His big boots sucked up a heavy mud, black and sticky, when he stepped off the sidewalk to let pass some farm woman with her baskets of vegetables hanging from her arms. He had lost his former keenness of eyesight; he stared at each person who passed with friendly insistence. His small eyes, prying, seeking, expressed his desire for and pleasure in renewed acquaintanceships. Frequently enough he greeted strangers, who became amused, and he concluded that he must have seen them somewhere and that he had done well not to ignore them. He passed the little Orthodox church and stopped at the edge of the sidewalk; he considered this building with its three onion-shaped domes especially pretty. It had been constructed in exactly the same style as the village churches of the Ukraine. Without envy he admitted that it was better than his own chapel. "But if you have the prettier church," he would tell the Orthodox priest, "I have the better parishioners." Ha! Ha! This mild joke made him laugh heartily at his own self-conceit. In all good faith, he agreed that there was room for both of them at Rorketon, and even for the clergyman of the United Church. His eyes, their corners creased by the sun and by his continuous smile, jumped from one sight to another, retaining with pleasure some always interesting characteristic of costume, of men's external appearance. He felt that he drew singularly close to God in this so fraternal a confusion of languages and faces.

He left the heart of the village and almost immediately was in the country. Deep in a field of wild mustard appeared his chapel and the one-room cabin which served him as presbytery. He stood still in contemplation before the two small structures behind their diminutive wooden bell tower which, because of its rustic shape and its plank roof, looked like a rural well. His heart lifted with pride. So satisfied was he with his parish that it was difficult for him not to talk about it constantly to everyone he met.

The Capuchin had been unable to restrain himself from pointing out its merits even to his Lordship the Bishop when he was making his rounds for confirmation. The Bishop had been deeply impressed. "Most unusual! Most ingenious!" the Bishop had remarked, yet he was relieved that his diocese did not contain a dozen more priests like the Capuchin. With these friars from Belgium, dependent directly on their convent in Louvain, rather than wholly under his own obedience, you had to expect peculiarities. A bit more, and these gallant monks would take to the roads and gather together the fishermen of Lakes Winnipegosis and Manitoba, as once had happened in Galilee. Now what was good for one age was not necessarily good for another.... But the Bishop was unperturbed. There were few of the Capuchin's kind. There always had been few.

Meanwhile Father Joseph-Marie had cut across the fields to the house of his neighbour, Mrs Macfarlane, with the excuse of borrowing some salt from her to put on his cold potatoes. Truth to tell, he did not easily reconcile himself to solitude. At times, when alone, he was visited by a keen feeling of distress, the sadness of having done nothing for God or for His creatures.

IV

The nine o'clock High Mass began, and step by step the Capuchin once again rehearsed in his mind the near-miracle he had brought to pass at Rorketon. A trifle worried, he waited for the noble tone of the harmonium to respond to his tremulous voice; much as he loved music, he chanted abominably off-key. And the ancient foot-bellows cried out for air and the air welled into music.

That harmonium was a whole story in itself!

Mrs Macfarlane had had it in her parlour for almost ten years, and never before had it served to render anything but Methodist hymns, lovely as they were, especially those written by Charles Wesley, the reformer's brother. Next to Gregorian chant, no music seemed to the old Capuchin more likely to please God than these poetic verses, which were always comparing Him to a harvester and giving Him thanks for the ripe corn, the full barns, the fertile earth. That Charles Wesley had been a sincere man, no doubt about it. All the same, how Father Joseph-Marie, when he paid a neighbourly call on Mrs Macfarlane, would have loved to hear that Protestant harmonium accompany some fine Catholic melody! Mrs Macfarlane had an only daughter, Aggie, who was no longer very young; she must have been about forty. Yet to Mrs Macfarlane she ever remained "delicate little Aggie." She fell sick. At the outset it did not seem serious: some stiffness in the joints, headaches, slight fever. The local doctor happened to be away at a medical meeting. In his wanderings, Father Joseph-Marie had seen many dreadful diseases in their first, insignificant symptoms; those headaches, the difficulty Aggie seemed to have in breathing looked to him like bad signs. So he insisted on Aggie's being taken to the Winnipegosis hospital. At first mother and daughter would have none of it; then they had had to yield to a forceful man in whom they could barely recognize the old Catholic priest, so peremptory, overbearing, and authoritative had he become. Aggie had indeed fallen prey to infantile paralysis. The Capuchin set in motion mysterious influences in Winnipeg; he secured an iron lung which was rushed north. If today Aggie could walk with only a cane to help her, she and her mother naturally thanked the Capuchin for it. As for him, he still laughed at the good joke played on Protestant Aggie Macfarlane who, without her having had the least suspicion of it, was cured by Saint Joseph, of whom he had secretly asked this favour. How the two women would have been riled had they learned what they owed to a saint with whom they had no acquaintance and of whom, truth to tell, they were highly suspicious!

Obviously it was more convenient for them to show

their gratitude directly to the priest himself, little as he deserved it. For a long while they had been trying to get him to divulge what he would like best.

How could he ever have told them that for months he had had his eye on their harmonium! It was true that Mrs Macfarlane no longer played it, because of her poor hands, twisted with arthritis. All the more reason to induce her to keep her harmonium, which as long as it stood there in the parlour might encourage Mrs Macfarlane to get better. Father Joseph-Marie blushed even at the thought of the unkind conjectures he sometimes entertained. "And yet, supposing Mrs Macfarlane were never to play again. Supposing . . . " He cast a very guilty glance at the harmonium. He had never been able to resolve himself to speak out, except that occasionally he asked whether the harmonium kept in good health, whether it had been an expensive instrument, and whether there was not danger that it might deteriorate more from the humidity if it remained so long out of use; he wasn't quite sure, himself, what was good for a harmonium; he was just wondering. He really thought he had never given himself away. And then it happened: "I've made a present of my harmonium," Mrs Macfarlane informed him one evening. "Oh! indeed," he had replied with deep sorrow. "That's a handsome gift, a very handsome gift. The person who received it must be very happy."

A little later he entered his chapel, heart heavy with envy, however hard he tried to banish the emotion. As for her parting with the harmonium, if truly she was getting rid of it, why should Mrs Macfarlane not have given it to him, who needed it so badly! The chapel was dark; almost as he stepped across the threshold, the Capuchin knocked into something. He struck a match, and what did he see installed in the very place where he had always imagined it – against the back wall – but Mrs Macfarlane's harmonium!

Alas! this present, which must so greatly have rejoiced the Capuchin, almost from the outset had planted in him another desire, even more exacting. Where, now, would he find the excellent musician, the perfect musician, to play the harmonium! Among the women of his parish there was not a single one who knew how at once to pedal, touch the keys, and turn the pages of a score – in a word, how to make music. He looked around, he asked questions, he rushed about. Man of little faith! He had been capable of suspecting that God, having given him a harmonium, would leave him with no one to play it.

And yet now, at this very moment, the Capuchin, as he turned around with his hands parted, saw at the back of the chapel the ever slightly exalted glance which characterized Kathy Macgregor when she communicated by means of music with the Eternal Principle. The Scotch woman's nostrils contracted. Her glasses cast back at the sun a brief burst of golden light. Her big hat jiggled. Quickly she opened flat the score and pedalled full speed ahead, having shoved back the music stool with her hips so as to give herself ample space before attacking Handel's Largo. His heart rejoicing, Father Joseph-Marie turned back toward the altar.

How Kathy Macgregor happened to be sitting at Mrs Macfarlane's harmonium in the Catholic chapel the Capuchin himself no longer fully remembered. What of it! Here was another of those tricks the good Lord likes to play. Kathy Macgregor was Rorketon's best musician, and probably the best in all the lake country. She was also its most convinced Presbyterian, striving to maintain, by herself alone if necessary, the full rigour of the reformed church. One day when they happened to meet in the general store, the conversation between the Capuchin and Kathy had worked its way to the religious slackness of the times. Truth to tell, the Capuchin saw no reason for his getting into a rage; it was Kathy who was really out of temper. As for that, the Capuchin would rather have chatted about music. Kathy, however, had been heavyhearted ever since the region's few Presbyterians had joined forces with the Congregationalists and the Methodists to form the United Church. That people whose ancestors had had the privilege of listening to the great Knox's thunder should have sunk to going out on Sundays after church was over, even to playing baseball! What sort of religion was this! Everything was licit, from automobile races on the Lord's Day to tobacco, liquor, and card playing! The minister himself played dominoes. At the rate they were going, they would soon be giving dances, such as she had heard tell they were already holding in the basement of the Winnipeg Kirk, and why not in the very Kirk itself? Since this was the state of affairs, Kathy preferred to make her own arrangements with God in her own parlour, with her old family Bible and the curtains well drawn against the world's tumult.

Now, right in the midst of her explosion, Kathy stopped short to take a better look at the Capuchin. With his long, sparse beard, his shabby robes, his thin cheeks, the monk struck her as on the whole not unlike the great Knox himself, from the descriptions she as a small girl had heard of this aged itinerant preacher, who travelled in fair weather and foul to every nook and corner of Scotland, urging austerity. She kept looking at the Capuchin, and the more she looked, the more she saw superimposed on the missionary's features the stern visage of Knox. All in all, this old Catholic priest might be the closest thing to Knox in all that region. It would be quite possible for him, too, were the occasion to arise, to tramp barefoot to frivolous Mary Stuart's court, there to inveigh against licentiousness.

"Do you drink?" she had asked him point-blank.

"Heavens, no," the Capuchin had replied, "my stomach won't stand it."

"As far as I know, you have no car, like those clergymen of today who go by comfortably leaning against their plush cushions, and who honk away with their horns to chase decent folk off the road?"

"Ha! Ha! Not even a bicycle, my poor Kathy. In the long run it's more convenient. I take advantage of other travellers, who keep going and coming. I can almost always get a lift."

"Very good!" Kathy had approved.

This elderly man did not play cards, either. He admitted that cards confused him. He had only one failing: he smoked coarse, strong tobacco. And yet he lived like a hermit in his cabin at Rorketon. Even though she had claimed that she came to better terms with God in her own parlour, in fact Kathy suffered from seeking Him in solitude. Less purposeful than she appeared, she thought she had noticed that God withdrew Himself from a soul too haughty, too alone. And, perhaps more than anything else, she missed lifting herself toward the Lord through the resplendent music of Handel and of Bach. No longer could she play at the United Church services; her conscience prevented her. But in that tiny plank chapel, so poor, at the very edge of the village! She dimly felt that in this town here was the best means to confound the proud and thus carry out the teachings of the great Knox.

Just then, with that sublime absence of mind which often served him better than any careful scheme, Father Joseph-Marie had quietly begun to talk – off-hand, without the least ulterior motive – of the parable of the talents, of those which began to bear fruit, and of those which lay dormant, buried in the earth. And thus God had acted upon Kathy's conscience. No need of probing deeper to find the reason for her presence that morning in the chapel or for the progress she had made since she had begun playing for the Catholics!

"*Ite missa est* . . . ," intoned Father Joseph-Marie.

The bell began to swing in its small wooden bell tower next the chapel, and it spread abroad a curious tocsin which recalled a passing locomotive more than it indicated the end of Sunday Mass in the country, during the season of hay and the wild rose. You might almost have thought it was a general alarm. Nor was this surprising. For Father Joseph-Marie's bell was a Canadian Pacific Railway bell, and before arriving to announce Rorketon's missions, it had long clanged atop that company's locomotives as they drew near some village or, in the midst of the prairie, at grade crossings in order to induce the grazing herds to move away from the tracks.

And this is how the Capuchin had obtained this bell, as well as all the other bells you might hear ring at each of his chapels.

When he had first reached Canada, fifteen years earlier, Father Joseph-Marie landed at Quebec, in his heedlessness and simplicity of mind unaware that his order had a house in that city. He had found himself a cheap room in a third-rate hotel, very near the railway station. At all hours trains came and went and shunted about in the yards. The big locomotive bells rang all the time. Deeply impressed, the Capuchin had remarked to himself: "I have found the most pious city in all the world. People are at their prayers the whole night through. I've never seen such a thing. Now that must be the bell of a convent of Poor Clares; I can just see the good nuns, their hands tucked in their sleeves, gliding toward their cold chapel at this late hour, there to pray God on behalf of the world's sinners. . . . And that – it sounds more austere – must be the bell of a Trappist monastery. . . . What piety there is in this city!" In the voices of all these bells, he heard a reproach of sorts for the missionary's vocation he had chosen. The highest perfection, perhaps, dwelt in pure contemplation. Endlessly to pray for mankind, just simply to pray – was that not the better choice? This disturbance of his conscience and a deep exaltation coupled with a feeling of exile had prevented the Capuchin's sleeping during this first night in Canada. He would doze off an instant and at once the clangour of a bell would reawaken in him the great debate. Would he not do better to ask the Pope for permission to enter a contemplative order? The bell grew still, but another, further away, began to strike. Yet other monks or nuns who were arising for prayer! Pure and pious little town of Quebec!

In every place he stopped, on the stages of his journey

to the backlands that summoned him, he had always, at once through attraction and through economy, slept near the railroad station, and always the Capuchin had heard the same nocturnal call to prayer. In the end he suspected that no country could be so continually fervent from one end to the other. And at last, in Winnipeg, he learned that the locomotives in this strange Canada were equipped with bells as well as with whistles. A few years later, when Rorketon's diminutive bell tower was tenantless, he remembered all this. The Capuchin had a stroke of genius; he left for Winnipeg and rushed to the office of the Canadian Pacific Railway's president.

"Mr Macdonald," the priest told him, "thanks to the bells on your trains, I long believed that God, in his very great mercy, had brought me to the world's most devout country."

He recounted the story of his first night at Quebec, the dilemma that had beset his faith. What, indeed, was the superior way: to serve God through action or through prayer alone? Truly, a major dilemma. God being all-powerful, was it not wiser to conclude that he could do without the collaboration of our deeds and that prayer was more pleasing to him? A disturbing dilemma, and all because of the locomotive bells.

They had brought him, the Capuchin avowed, one of his life's greatest religious emotions. He had believed that the city and the whole country were animated by a faith such as had not been seen since the Middle Ages – if then! He had had somewhat to change his tune since. Still, the people really were devout. Thus had his Rorketon parishioners, poor Ukrainians, Icelanders, and Ruthenians, truly bled themselves white to build a chapel and presbytery. And everything was going splendidly.

"I have an organist of your communion, I imagine – a Presbyterian lady," the Capuchin had carefully pointed out. "I have a Protestant catechism teacher, the Rorketon schoolmistress who, I declare, teaches doctrine from the Quebec lesser catechism fully as well as I could do it myself. God has accomplished many things at Rorketon," concluded the Capuchin. "However, we as yet have no bell."

At this point in his narrative, the priest had most innocently allowed the purpose of his call to become obvious. What did the CPR do, he inquired, with cracked or rusty bells, in a word with bells that had grown old in service?

But that never happened, Mr Macdonald had informed him, with great difficulty suppressing his mirth. CPR bells never wore out. They neither cracked nor rusted. They were made to last a hundred years and more.

"Oh!" Father Joseph-Marie looked most vexed.

"How many bells would you need?" Mr Macdonald had asked him.

Father Joseph-Marie had been on the point of replying three or four, discounting the future. But he had stopped himself in time: "I have only one small belfry ready. . . . "

"Well, then," Mr Macdonald had promised, "for each of your bell towers you will receive a bell from the company."

And so it happened that that morning the CPR was ringing out God's glory, while Kathy Macgregor, who had been practising it for three weeks, at last launched forth on Bach's great Toccata and Fugue. Mrs Macfarlane's aged harmonium was furnished with a whole row of buttons which controlled its lower register and its treble stops. Kathy pulled one of these out, struggling with it a bit, for the mechanism was no longer very pliant; the felt which surrounded certain stops had folded back on itself; she pushed another in and, since she was not tall and her legs were on the short side, she had to contort herself violently in order to accomplish all this without rising from the music bench and ceasing to pump, with her flat-shod feet, air into the old instrument, which wheezed in its deeper tones.

The moment she was a bit less preoccupied, Kathy raised her eyes heavenward, let them soar an instant, her eyeballs revolving high in their sockets. Then she was preparing for the loveliest passages, her head bent very low, one hand hovering over the keyboard, her nostrils quivering, her eyes shut, as though the better to savour within herself the whole of the passage she was playing. And then – a hop and a skip – and both her hands were racing over the keys.

Oh! the bell, the Bach Toccata and Fugue, the exquisite sunlight you could see through the open door, dancing over the mustard fields! The Capuchin, having divested himself of his chasuble, was joyfully striding down the aisle of the tiny church to join the group of faithful, almost all of whom were lingering around the harmonium, fascinated as much by Kathy's efforts as by the effect she produced through them.

The last notes lingered long in the fine, warm silence which, immediately after the Toccata and Fugue, filled the small church.

"Ah! my dear Kathy," exclaimed the Capuchin, "you played better than ever!"

With perfect sincerity he told her the same thing every Sunday throughout the mission. Kathy passed a good portion of the week in the empty chapel practising not merely what she knew but liturgical melodies wholly novel to her and which surprised her with their richness. To the reward, bracing in itself, of having put Rorketon's backsliding Presbyterians in their place, there was added for Kathy that of a full appreciation of her talents – sweet indeed to a musical soul. At least the Capuchin did not confuse Bach with Czerny's exercises. She was growing fonder and fonder of the bearded old man.

They passed through the open door. The small wooden bell tower still shook from the labours of the ringer, who was now pulling the rope with less and less violence. The parishioners looked dignified in their Sunday best. The exquisite music bathed in its own greatness the departure of this small group of Christians who, the very moment they stepped down from the stoop, found themselves knee-high in the tall, yellowing grass. Almost all of them in black, their trousers baggy, the men walked through the hay and wild mustard, and they twisted their broad-brimmed hats in their heavy hands, still hesitant to put them on their heads. The women were just beginning to move out, after the men had gone some little distance, in accordance with the decorum current in many Manitoba Catholic parishes. Lined up on the telephone wires, small birds, which Kathy's flights of harmony had put on their mettle, sang their hearts out.

"Oh, dear Kathy!" cried the Capuchin. "If ever anyone on earth beheld the Lord, it was our Johann Sebastian!"

It was the loveliest Sunday he had ever spent at Rorke-ton. There was nothing left for him to desire. He had, in this mission, gathered together everything which could give God pleasure. Or – better – was it not God who had here taken up His abode as it pleased Him?

Yet the more the heart is sated with joy, the more it becomes insatiable.

v

That same Sunday was the day of Rorketon's great Ukrainian festival. It took place under Orthodox auspices, since the latter were more numerous than the Catholics of Greek Rite and hence possessed a meeting hall next door to the smithy. Orthodox and Catholics, moreover, gladly mingled on this occasion in order to celebrate in sufficiently large number, and beneath the portrait of their national poet, Chevtchenko, their common Ukraine. For the needs of the cause, people in this so sparsely populated lake country indeed had at times to ally themselves if they wanted to stage a festival that would look like a festival, and the Capuchin approved this necessity; he regretted that throughout the rest of the year, with no sufficient motive for understanding, people of the same national origin had to go their separate ways.

Seated at the banquet table and surrounded by young

Ukrainian girls, the priest sampled complex dishes without too clearly recognizing their ingredients. There would have been a rich beet soup served with sour cream, cabbage with various sauces, but always wrapped in pastry – these tartlets were called *piroshki* – delicious rolls covered with caraway seeds, and again cabbage, creamed and sour, likewise in an envelope of pastry.

Everything was very good, the Capuchin assured the young women who were serving him. He would have been put to it to say what he had eaten.

The speeches began. The president of the United Ukrainian Society led off. Taras Simonovski by name, he was a Rorketon notary, in his spare time a literary man, and the motive force of the Ukrainian festival as well as the Ukrainian library in process of establishment at Rorketon. Hence he was the very person to undertake the task he had set himself: to prove that Gogol, often claimed by the Russians as a Russian author, in truth belonged to them the Ukrainians. Gogol had been born in the Ukraine, at Sorotchinzi in the Government of Poltava. The people applauded. Anton Gusaliuk, Rorketon schoolteacher, spoke on Ukrainian folklore, while Gregori Stupovitch, as he did each year, dealt with the great historical question. All the United Ukrainian Society's members who had some degree of learning and education, or were to any extent outstanding, such as the photographer Simon Satlura, "Specialist in Photographing Weddings, Banquets, and Ukrainian Marriages," as he advertised himself on the sign over his Main Street shop – five personages in all – addressed an audience of about eighty. But Gregori Stupovitch was the most awe-inspiring; several Rorketon Ukrainians who subscribed to the newspaper printed in their language at Winnipeg had remarked therein and called each other's attention to the name of Gregori Stupovitch affixed to a two-column article. This published article was the very same text as Gregori was now reciting, having committed every word of it to memory.

The flies buzzed, the heat was stifling in the crowded hall, yet the white-kerchiefed women, the peasants from the surrounding countryside, almost all illiterate, most of them never having opened a book in their lives, listened in warm, intent immobility. Some kept their mouths half open, as though to suck in the long, tiresome speech. Down the wrinkled cheeks of an old woman tears trickled.

When were these short, thick-set, quiet men, these women with their long, bony faces, really themselves? During the three hundred and sixty-four days of the year when they scratched and toiled, stubborn, ambitious to increase their possessions, and above all jealous of him among them who succeeded? Or else on the three hundred and sixty-fifth day, when they sat side by side, their countenances lifted confidently toward the notary Taras Simonovski, who so often swindled them? And as for that, when he was telling the truth? Every day, while extorting a big fee from one of his compatriots and claiming: "Now, I'm making you a special rate . . . "? Or at the Ukrainian festival, where he asked for nothing for himself, yet insisted: "We Ukrainians should stick together in our business if we want to remain Ukrainian"?

Father Joseph-Marie smiled in his beard. Such were men's hearts – men who were often squabbling and vindictive, but basically so guileless that they could believe themselves friends by lining up under the symbol of a republic which had existed only for a day or two! High talk, then, was not too bad a beginning for a festival dedicated to friendship.

Nonetheless, the most pacific of these talks occasionally included matter to which some slight objection might be taken. Thus events in the Ukraine during the autumn of 1917 had not taken place precisely as Gregori Stupovitch asserted. The Capuchin imagined the consternation were he suddenly to arise and say his say: "Forgive me, Gregori Stupovitch," he might remark. "I was myself in those parts at the time of the proclamation of a free and independent Ukraine, and are you always quite certain about what you are saying? . . . "

He began to laugh silently, shaking his shoulders. Ha! Ha! The poor people were already mixed up enough as it was by what Gregori was telling them without his intruding his own version upon their consideration.

Then too, the singing was about to begin; the chorus was assembling, and the Capuchin in his great enthusiasm was the first to applaud it.

In front of the group of singers, who stood in two rows, the leader took his stand, bowing slightly right and left. He was none other than Anton Gusaliuk, the schoolteacher, the very one who had just given so good an account of Ukrainian folklore. There was almost nothing Ukrainian left about this Anton Gusaliuk except his name, and for the English-speaking he had even transformed it into Tony. He wore a tiny, well-trimmed moustache, black-rimmed glasses, and a blue serge suit. He was thin and desiccated, and the top of his head was bald. He was the image of the village schoolteacher who has put intellectual preoccupations on a higher level than heavy work and brawn. He had no trace of an accent, at least when speaking English. Rather was it his parents' language that he massacred.

His old mother was in the audience. She had given birth to this one of her sons, her little Anton, at the edge of the wheat field, one evening when she was hastening to gather the sheaves. Neither she nor her old Gusaliuk had ever had time to crack a book. Anton, however, scarcely resembled them at all, either in their build, their accent, or their ignorance; and Anton's two aged parents, tucked away at the back of the hall, she under her kerchief knotted peasant fashion, he with his long, ragged moustaches, gleamed with pride. Thinking it over, the Capuchin smiled with sympathy. Because here is what happened in the lake country when a son or daughter of Ukrainian immigrants scarcely bore any resemblance to them. This son or daughter one fine day took notice – in an aesthetic way – of the poetry, the warmth, the picturesqueness of the ancient folklore. The young people staged an operetta in the Ukrainian language; they formed a choral society; they learned from the old people the dances of former days now largely forgotten; they put on a great festival, and their poor aged parents heard talk to their hearts' content about the Ukraine, which they had thought it their duty to forget for progress's sake.

With a curt nod of his head Anton gave the signal to begin. The ten voices of the chorus soared into the nervous, sparkling song of the mulberry bush. The Capuchin lifted his chair and turned it in such fashion as better to see the front of the hall. He settled back again, his habit stretched wide across his spread knees, his hands resting there as on a tablecloth. His bearded features sparkled. He devoured with his eyes the small group of singers clad in their national costume. At the edge of his eyelids a tear already trembled.

An ardent love for the joys of this world, regret at thinking that he would surely have to leave it while he yet hungered for them, at the same time a desire for the absolute, to find himself at last face to face with God – all these emotions the highly sensuous song of the mulberry bush strangely stimulated in the priest's heart.

A young girl separated herself from the group; she stepped forward and with pretty gestures of the hands, now pressed against her heart, now held out to the public, with her skirt swinging and her eyes flashing, she began singing solo the song of the mulberry bush. However gifted the voices of the choristers and, generally, those of all the young Rorketon Ukrainians, to whom singing came naturally, this voice incomparably surpassed them.

"Loubka Koussilevska! Loubka Koussilevska!" the name fluttered about the room, from mouth to mouth. Of course she must be the surprise of which Taras Simonovski had spoken, and later Anton Gusaliuk, and which was worth its weight in gold. Even the toothless old peasant women drew themselves up straight in pride at being able to lay claim to this Ukrainian talent.

As for the Capuchin, he looked enchanted. His lips were parted; on his chest his reddish beard rose and fell in rhythm with his quick breathing. All his life's joys came back to him at the same moment; he was overwhelmed at encountering so much happiness: the beautiful years passed in this lake country and, before that, his long jaunts over Europe, Kiev and Odessa, which he had seen with his own eyes, and what lovely cities! and how had God indulged his appetite for travel! Truly, music apart, nothing opens the heart so much as journeying from one land to another; here was the best way to understand peoples; and was it conceivable that he had himself beheld, in his own lifetime, so many of the beauties of this earth! This being so, he would never, in all his life, be able to thank God adequately. Thanks for music, above all, that language of Heaven and, of course, for his bells, for his harmonium and the good Kathy! Swollen with gratitude, the Capuchin's soul thus quite naturally lay open to desire for even more. Loubka's charming voice, which so turned your heart toward God, how well it would sound in the Rorketon chapel!

Obviously, he conceded, it was already a wonderful business to have the harmonium and a musician like Kathy at his disposal; he must not seem ungrateful, tire God with too many demands. However, was it not clear that if God had already supplied him with the instrument and the musician, it was expressly to add thereto Loubka Koussilevska's soprano! Just as the harmonium had called for a musician, did not the musician now call for a voice to sing solo? And as for that, would not this individual voice eventually lead to a choir?

He imagined his Children of Mary, all five of them, grouped at the back of the chapel and following the lead of Loubka's small hand. It was she who would render the "Panis Angelicus." And what lovely marriage ceremonies he would be able to offer! It had always saddened him not to be able to have marriages with music. On such occasions Loubka would sing Schubert's "Ave Maria." Another tear spilled over, so greatly was he pleased by what he glimpsed. Too bad that it was not yet fully accomplished. At the notion that he must eliminate from his pretty picture the choir and perhaps even Loubka herself, his heart ached. Kathy and the harmonium by themselves already seemed to him somewhat less satisfying.

Of a sudden he began staring hopefully at the young Ukrainian singer; the happy idea flashed through his mind that he had already seen her somewhere: was it among the Catholics of the Greek Rite? Were that the case, she would take no objection to singing in his chapel. The very next Sunday he was there on mission! He saw his small church packed. People everywhere – filling the pews along the main aisle and the side pews too. Kathy would play a lovely chord. And the moment would come when he, no longer able to contain himself, would also offer his faithful "a surprise worth its weight in gold." Ha! Ha! Loubka Koussilevska! he exclaimed to himself in the gay tone of someone who has just played a good joke. And convinced from then on that she was on the road to becoming one of his parishioners, he discovered in her even greater talent and the voice of an angel.

"Bravo!" he cried out.

It had become impossible for him to repress his admiration. His exclamations, mingled with the clicking of his tongue, distracted the audience, which turned toward the corner whence came all this noise. Now the Capuchin gestured broadly, urging them to listen to Loubka in silence, while he himself continued to mumble.

"Ho! Ho!" the Capuchin would say. "A voice of gold! The most beautiful voice I've heard in a long while! Bravo!"

On the platform, the young girls and boys were clasping each other's hands, then wheel, then strike the floor sharply with your heel; they were performing a heady Caucasian dance. Eyes were shining; the fine embroidery on their blouses sparkled; their short skirts whirled like tops, red, green, orange, blue; at last all the colours commingled, while tiny leather boots of red or tan bounded faster and faster.

Then a young lad danced the Cossack *trepak*, his legs crisscrossing beneath him at lightning speed, his forelock slapping against his forehead. Rising from time to time, with one knee half bent, he would kick out hard with his heel, as though to strike something, and at the same instant a cry would burst from his chest – harsh, wild, frenzied.

All this while the Capuchin, his hands slipped into his sleeves, ruminated on his schemes for Masses with music. If only they would hurry up with their festival! Despite his appearance of calm, a strange nervousness warned him that so great a joy would escape him were he not quick in grasping it.

His eyes, half delighted, half put out of patience, seemed to want to hasten the pace of dances already frantically fast. Through this whirlwind he saw his choir, with Loubka singing the "Ave Maria" of Schubert.

How eager he was to talk with her, to come to an understanding with her, and to behold at last fully realized that which was even then so well launched toward success!

And thus everything would be settled with her before he left, later that week, for his most remote mission where, unhappily, the times were not yet ripe for sacred song.

VI

At Portage des Prés he carried on a business far removed from music, and which might have been judged wholly irrelevant to the duties of his ministry. But, as the Capuchin saw it, it was quite useless to preach God's justice on earth were he not to busy himself with certain things closely linked thereto as, for example and in this place, the fur trade.

Thus had it happened that the Capuchin was at war with the merchant Bessette.

He would alight in front of the General Store, most frequently from the postman Ivan Bratislovski's rickety old carriage, sometimes from a buckboard, occasionally from the automobile of an obliging travelling salesman who had carried him to his destination. He stepped knee-high into grass and was instantly in the toils of a wild, hot breeze which billowed the skirts of his habit and made the telephone wires hum, their passage through thirty-two miles of wilderness here come to its end. This was the northernmost human community before you reached the Indian reservation. Father Joseph-Marie was always in a great hurry to get to this settlement, but on arrival his joy was spoiled by the realization that in a brand-new mission, at its very start, he had succeeded in making himself an enemy.

Some years earlier, Eustache Bessette had held undisputed sway over the largely halfbreed population of Portage des Prés. At first glance you might have thought Bessette's kingdom almost uninhabited. It was a low plain, infinitely melancholy, over which, swayed the ragged plumes of water grasses that reached even into the village itself, to the door stoops of its five houses. You could enter and leave the settlement in the time needed to take one long breath. Before the wild hay had been mown, however, you could readily make out the wheel tracks running through it; they led to puny tufts of dwarf birch and spindly poplar. Each small natural hiding place in this open country sheltered its trapper's cabin. Not one of them stood openly in sight, along the main trail, as though such a position would have entailed too great an exposure to curiosity. Many of these cabins were used only for a portion of the year. With the coming of winter, the trappers moved north, to catch squirrel, muskrat, mink, and ermine; some few wives accompanied their hunters; most of them joined forces to spend the winter in one cabin or another. Toward spring the men returned from

the tundra with their precious furs which Bessette bought
for a pittance. There were times when the trapper would
not know what his pelts were worth, but whether he knew
or not, he had to take Bessette's terms since he was the
only fur buyer in the area and, even more, since he had a
stranglehold over everyone through his system of selling
on credit.

This was the way it worked: all summer the poor
halfbreeds got deeper into the store's debt; salt pork, tea,
corn syrup, tobacco, a bit of cotton goods, too, for the
women's dresses – everything was charged to their
accounts. Now the halfbreed, so poorly equipped to
understand the value of hard cash, was utterly at a loss to
comprehend what went on in the storekeeper's mind or –
it came to the same thing – what went on in his account
books. Thus all summer long Eustache Bessette urged
them to spend. "Don't you fancy this percale that's just
come in, Samson? It's what the women are wearing in
town. Take it. Pay me later." Later, for the halfbreed,
amounted to never.

In the spring, when the fur began to come in, Bessette
changed his tactics. He needed his money right away. The
halfbreeds had been spendthrift – so much the worse for
them. Now was the time to settle. The price of fur had
gone down. "I'll give you so much and not a cent more."

It was an easy and most satisfactory system. In many
places it had sufficed to enslave whole populations of
hunters and fishermen to the advantage of a single individual. Sooner or later competition would disrupt this fine
state of affairs; Bessette greatly feared it, and he was hurry-
ing, against this evil day, to round out his fortune. The
profits of a year or two might be enough to turn the trick;
Bessette asked no more than a couple of years, when
Father Joseph-Marie came upon the scene.

It happened one May evening in Bessette's store. Samson Mackenzie was showing the merchant his catch. Suspicious, hair-splitting, his pencil perched on his ear, the fur
king was looking for every blemish he could find, real or

imaginary. This skin had been ripped by a badly set trap; this other pelt was of most inferior quality. Last winter's mink was below par. The purpose of all this was to justify himself in offering a piddling price.

Poor Samson noticed the Capuchin, who was silently smoking his big pipe near the stove; he cast a disconsolate glance at the priest, pleading to him for help.

"Show me your furs, Samson." He had some little knowledge in this field, though he was no expert. Samson's fur seemed to him exceptional in the darkness of its sheen. Father Joseph-Marie sucked at his pipe and shook his head; what was needed here was another merchant, be it Jew or Christian, to stimulate business. The missionary stroked his beard dejectedly. For the pure pleasure of defying Bessette he would have bought some fur on the spot, had he had the necessary cash. Instead a simpler plan occurred to the Capuchin. Not even a plan, really. Just an idea.

"If you want to trust me with your pelts, Samson my friend, I'll make it my business to find a buyer who pays decent prices."

The halfbreed has a ready imagination. He could quickly bridge the gap between this half-promise and the certainty of rich profit. The news spread from trapper to trapper that the Capuchin had a definite buyer in mind, most likely an Englishman, who would give fabulous prices. After Mass next day, each of them piled his finest skins at the priest's feet. A few of them respectfully called him "Your Lordship, *Monseigneur*," which vastly annoyed the missionary. "I am not a bit Your Lordship, thank God!" he protested vehemently.

To no avail. The halfbreeds continued to bring him pelts and then more pelts, greeting him with extreme politeness, "Here, Lordship."

They abbreviated it, pronouncing it "Tigneur," and thus smoothed away his annoyance.

What was he to do with all those skins? He could never transport the three or four bales they constituted. Nevertheless he departed, laden like a Jewish pedlar. Whenever he had to walk, he carried his great precious burden on his own shoulders. His boldness was beginning to make him take thought. Was it not against the rule of his community to wander about with perhaps two hundred dollars' worth of goods? As a matter of fact, what would be the precise value of the big bale he was lugging with him? The Capuchin had much higher figures in the back of his head. It might even go as high as five hundred dollars. He began to be fearful of moths, water, highwaymen – he who had always had so firm a trust in mankind.

He arrived at Rorketon and, half absent-mindedly, half purposely, instead of taking the road toward his convent, the Capuchin headed for the railway station. Thus it happened that he found himself with his furs on the Winnipeg train, bound for he knew not whither, metamorphosed, if you please, into a merchant. Wholly novel cares assailed him, and they prevented him from praying in peace. Even the night before he had slept with one eye open, the furs piled on his bed. In the morning he at first could not locate the bundle, for it had disappeared under the comforter. Fear had overcome him, and for the first time in his life his thoughts when he awakened had not been directed toward God.

Now he looked to Providence for help. He had placed himself in such a position as regards God's care that surely God could not fail to extricate him from it.

He reached the city and, always mingling absence of mind with confidence, he went to see a Main Street fur merchant, who offered him a price already far higher than Bessette's. Now, however, his madness and his enthusiasm made the Capuchin raise his sights. "No sale!" said he. All the same he did sell a few furs in Winnipeg, enough to buy a railway ticket without seeing too clearly how deeply he was to become involved. And so he found himself on a Canadian transcontinental train with Toronto as his destination.

In this city, Canada's second largest, Father Joseph-

Marie, his mind fresh and with no experience to hamper him, after only two days' search ended up, having encountered no real obstacles, at the Imperial Fur Company. All he had done was to ask directions and advice from seven or eight persons, strangers, of course, and hence having no interest in putting him on the wrong track. Since he had thus, by himself alone, eliminated all the middlemen between the trapper and the gods of the industry, the Imperial Fur Company's first offer stopped him dead in his tracks.

"A thousand dollars!"

"A thousand dollars," repeated the Capuchin, overwhelmed with fright at the thought that he had been gallivanting around for days with such valuable baggage, not even insured against theft, fire, or any other sort of damage. A thousand dollars! He bared his teeth in anger against Bessette. A thousand dollars! What then was worth the mass of furs he had left behind at Portage des Prés if this, a mere sample, was worth a thousand dollars!

This reflection gave the Capuchin's features a look of profound hesitation. He began to think about his Superior, whom he had not even informed of this trip. His face took on an expression of guilt, of remorse and, finally, of a total renunciation of this world's business.

"Eleven hundred dollars!" offered Sam Goldie, fearful lest the Capuchin might slip through his hands.

"What!" said the missionary in an even more astounded tone of voice, which could readily have been mistaken for indignation.

"One thousand two hundred dollars," Goldie suggested, "but that's my last offer. Ever since they have been organized, the furriers and dyers get preposterous wages. Damage insurance premiums have tripled." In short, he gave so many excuses that Father Joseph-Marie rightly judged that he could obtain a price better than that which had at first so astounded him.

Moreover, he was taking to this game with passionate

delight. He would have bargained for hours now to squeeze out an additional hundred dollars.

"Those skins you have in your hands," he undertook to explain, "are mink of the great North. They are not taken from the puny, sickly bodies of beasts raised in captivity where they waste away, losing their appetites and the sheen of their coats in some miserable cage. Not degenerate mink . . . just feel that gloss of freedom, the sheen of animals you have to go far to get. . . . Indeed, have you any idea how far you have to go to find such skins? You have to go up lakes and rivers, carry your supplies on your own back across portages, journey as far as Lake Katimik, Chetk Lake, Lake Braken, and even beyond. In an aeroplane," said he with an emphasis marked by a friendly smile, "it's not too tiring. And wonderful country, too. A couple of years ago I had the good luck to fly over it. From far off, like that, seen from the air, the North doesn't look so difficult, you know! But imagine yourself venturing on foot or in a canoe, in the dead of winter, through this tangle of small lakes and low timber. . . . "

"A thousand four hundred dollars, and that's absolutely my final price," said Goldie.

"I knew a poor fellow," began the Capuchin, "who in the end left his wretched bones somewhere along the shores of Red Deer Lake. I'm not going to tell you that sad story. Just imagine! A blizzard surprised my poor Oscar Chartrand as he was finishing the round of his traps. It was cold beyond belief. . . . "

"One thousand four hundred and fifty dollars!"

They settled for the round sum of fifteen hundred. Alarmed at an ambition which might carry him too far and bring him low, like the scheming little girl who dropped her milk jug on her way to market, Father Joseph-Marie rushed to the office and signed the sales contract.

Since that time he had acquired ease in his business dealings. The company as well as the halfbreeds had reason to congratulate themselves on account of the Capuchin. And the proof of it lay in that magnificent mink overcoat presented to Father Joseph-Marie with the thanks of the Imperial Fur Company.

So he arrived in Toronto each spring clad, externally at least, like an ancient Boyar. He hoped he was not committing the sin of pride. He wore the coat but once a year and solely on his visit to Sam Goldie. To sport this superb greatcoat before the poor Portage des Prés halfbreeds was out of the question. Justifiably the trappers might have thought that they had been done in by their missionary. Moreover, how could he go about preaching charity and the love of the poor garbed like an earthly despot! On the other hand, he did not wish to seem thankless to the donors of the mink coat. The Imperial Fur Company had had a good impulse, and if it could please their people to dress an old missionary like a bishop, it was not up to him to deprive them of this small satisfaction.

This, then, is the way the Capuchin solved the problem of the overcoat.

He left it at Winnipeg in a mothproof cover with a Hungarian woman of his acquaintance. He departed from Toutes Aides in his ancient sheepskin – which he wore with the fleece inside and the cloth out, because the cloth, after all, was less worn than the fleece – without gloves and with a heavy grey scarf wrapped five or six times around his neck. In Winnipeg took place the sea-change. To top it off, the Capuchin bought himself a cigar. He entered Goldie's place with his woodsman's stride, cigar clamped between his jaws, a folded newspaper under his arm, but still without gloves, his hands reddened by the cold. He had noticed that he got more and more satisfactory terms by arguing man to man, as a peer among peers. He did not light his cigar, the smoke of which would have asphyxiated him, but he nonchalantly shed his greatcoat. For a few days each year he relished the impression of being powerful and shrewd and the feeling of security afforded him by the fur coat. He recalled Gogol's fine story, "The

Overcoat," and he agreed that nothing could give you as
much self-confidence as rich clothing. God had done well
to deprive him of money. He could have been just as
proud as the next man. He held his head high even in
front of the president of the Imperial Fur Company.
Whether it were he or some other man, no one greatly
overawed the Capuchin when he was wearing his mink
coat. "Just feel the fineness and softness of that fur. Fur of
freedom! To get so warm and smooth a pelt the trappers
have to plunge two hundred miles into the North . . .
beyond Red Deer Lake. . . . "

The skins were now shipped direct from Portage des
Prés. The Capuchin went to Toronto only for the annual
contact, to discuss prices, the quantity of pelts, and sometimes even the trends of fashion, which leaned now
toward muskrat, now toward beaver. He had progressed
far beyond grabbing the cheque the moment it was signed,
as he had on his first visit. Cheques were sent in his name
to the Portage des Prés post office. And he himself left
Toronto like a big businessman who does not need to have
his pockets stuffed with bundles of bills in order to feel
wealthy. But wholly different was his attitude when he
would come, as on that very day, to present himself at the
window of the little cubicle in one corner of the general
store which served as post office and ask for his mail. For
him it was then the reverse of the medal.

"My mail. Would you be kind enough to give me my
mail, Monsieur Bessette?" the Capuchin politely asked.

The halfbreeds were waiting for their money, one seated
on a half-open bag of lentils, another on the counter itself,
swinging his heavy rubber boots. Samson, sitting back on
his heels, his fur hat shoved down on his ears, slyly
watched Bessette. He began to hum a tune packed with
mischief while at the same time whittling a small bit of
wood with the point of his pocketknife. Bessette took a
long while shifting from his status of merchant to that of

postmaster. He weighed out a pound of rice with the utmost procrastination.

"My mail, when you have time, Monsieur Bessette," the Capuchin once more requested.

In his own heart he thought the humiliation visited on the merchant Bessette most harsh. To have done him out of his best trading was quite enough; it was going too far to seem to rejoice at it. Yet how could he avoid it! He did not like to travel very far with a big cheque in his pocket; he had the habit of making squills to light his pipe out of any odd bits of paper he might find there. Prudence forced him to have the money sent to Portage des Prés and to distribute it the moment it arrived.

At last Bessette entered the cubicle. His soul was filled with bitterness. He himself had not the least doubt that the Capuchin was overjoyed at his triumph. Never trust the simpleminded look of those old missionaries! They talk to you about God and justice all day long, and they have nothing better to do than league themselves against the whites with those Indians and halfbreeds of theirs! What was needed here was a secular priest, such a pastor as they had everywhere else, who concerned himself only with religion – baptizing, hearing confessions, marrying people – and who left the merchants a free hand. He, Bessette, was so little against religion that he was ready to have a good priest's house built at his own expense, to give a large plot of ground, in return for a pastor who would mind his own business. He had hinted as much to the Bishop. Perhaps the ground under the Capuchin's feet was cut much further away than the old fellow suspected. Not even a Canadian, and the man thought he could rule the roost!

Bessette fingered the thin packet of letters, pretended that it took him a long time to find the one he had so quickly discovered, scrutinized, weighed.

"Look carefully," the Capuchin urged him. "My letter must be there."

Bessette was sweating. Great was his suffering when he

had to hand the priest the registered envelope with the Imperial Fur Company's name and address printed on its corner. He dreamed of the pleasure it would have given him to have thrown it into the fire.

Yet this was not the most cruel moment. The refinement of torture came when the good Father, glancing at the envelope's contents, whistled between his teeth with joy. Sometimes he could not help himself and read the figure out loud. "Three thousand dollars, my children!" The halfbreeds thronged around him. They wanted to see the cheque, touch it, examine it front and back. A mere tiny scrap of paper, covered with stamps, and just think what it represented!

When they had looked at the cheque to their hearts' content, the halfbreeds returned it to the Capuchin, who again addressed Bessette. He did it with an expression of sorrow. This pre-eminence with which Providence overwhelmed him was a heavy burden to bear. As though to extenuate it, he wound himself up in complex formulas: "If it doesn't bother you too much, if it doesn't put you out, I should be obliged if you would have the courtesy to cash this small cheque for me, Monsieur Bessette. Otherwise I should have to go to Sainte Rose du Lac."

Then did the merchant-postmaster fight a hard battle within himself. He was sorely tempted to send the Capuchin packing. But the indolent halfbreeds normally spent a good part of their money on the spot, at the place where they received it. To force them to go get it at Sainte Rose du Lac meant the sure sacrifice of handsome profits to the merchants down there.

Bessette began to count the bills. It was his habit to have them at hand, since in preparation for this business he had had the bank send him a large amount in cash. Nonetheless did it seem to him that here was his own money, his own life-blood, from which he was parting.

Yet the more the bills piled up on the wicker ledge, the more the Capuchin shrank within himself, the more he grew ill at ease. He was becoming sorrowful. So much money! For the best of men, is not money a stumbling block, a danger to the soul, often a cause of hardness of heart!

"Here's enough cash for them to drink themselves stupid," Bessette was whispering. "They'll head for town and squander it on all kinds of foolishness."

At first he had not known that his words touched the priest's most sensitive spot; now he was quite sure they did, and he rubbed them in: "If Ti-Pitte Mackenzie had not got fifteen hundred dollars in a lump sum last year, he wouldn't have rushed off to buy himself a Chevrolet at Winnipegosis, and he would not have rammed himself into a truck. A poor fellow who was driving for the first time in his life, and drunk in the bargain!"

The Capuchin bowed his head. He felt much more to blame than Bessette could ever imagine. Sad to say, it was all too true that in proportion as the trappers' incomes increased, they went in more heavily for drink, extravagant clothing for their wives, and the movies at Rorketon. He had thought to labour for their good, and he had perhaps succeeded only in drawing them away from it. Certainly it was not in men's power to create the happiness of others or even to allay injustice. Yet how sad at heart was he that he had not succeeded!

He sought asylum in his small chapel, situated a little way from the general store, in a clearing amidst scrawny poplars. He prepared himself to hear the trappers' confessions. They almost all bore the surnames either of Mackenzie or Parisien. In an earlier day a Scotch hunter, a great wanderer and great lover, had covered the Little Water Hen country from end to end and from top to bottom, leaving in many a cabin children born of the lively attraction the halfbreed women had felt for this hearty blond rover with the blue eyes. After his own fashion he had immortalized himself along the Little Water Hen. He had even frequented the Indian women on the reservation, and to that day there were Saultais who perpetuated the adventurer's name. So great was its prestige

among the Indians that when they were baptized and had
to choose a name to give them legal status, many of them
picked Mackenzie. For about the same reasons, a whole
clan of halfbreeds was called Parisien, but in this case
rather in memory of a nickname than a family name.
Long since had been forgotten the true name of the Pari-
sian who had ventured into the region, and perhaps it had
never been known, seeing that there were the best of
reasons for remembering it.

That evening Father Joseph-Marie was somewhat sor-
rowfully reflecting on the manner in which many human
beings are engendered, a manner in which love plays so
little part. These wretched halfbreeds, exploited from their
very origins, were still exploited by all sorts of pleasure-
vendors who took advantage of their innocence. They
were not equipped to handle too much money, not being
used to money's ways. "Yet if we have to wait," thought
the poor man, "until people know what to do with justice
and liberty, we might as well admit that they never will be
given them. Then, too, it is by its exercise that we learn
justice." But suppose he were wrong!

One doubt weighed heavily on him. Perhaps it was not
God who had recommended the Imperial Fur Company
to him, perhaps had not even guided him to Toronto. If
that were the case, however, he must have made that trip,
that improbable series of bargains on his own account!
Come, come! That was out of the question! God alone
could have achieved the bargain with Goldie. It was simply too soon to ask Him for explanations. And perhaps
with God we had to do without explanations. Otherwise,
what merit would there be in trusting Him!

He slipped the surplice and stole over his spotted old
habit. He felt himself a sheepish, clumsy old man, who
perhaps did more harm than good. Ever since the agree-
ment with the Imperial Fur Company, Bessette never put
foot inside the church. Meanwhile a great forbearance for
the merchant had come to being in the Capuchin's heart,
ever since he had himself experienced, once a year,

wrapped in his mink coat, the feeling of wealth. Poverty was not, perhaps, the only means of knowing others. To assume that it was would be to assume that in this world there existed only the poor.

"And then it was so pleasant," he ventured in further explanation, "to be the more powerful one on this earth, as art Thou, my God, in Heaven."

VII

Each year, some fine evening toward the third or last Sunday of July, one of the Tousignant children would dash up to the house crying, "Here's the Capuchin! The Capuchin's here!"

This visit occurred during the liveliest part of the summer on Little Water Hen island. July was the season for harvesting the wild hay which grew there abundantly. Bessette sent barges to collect it, which descended the Big Water Hen as far as the lake and from there made their way to Winnipegosis, where the hay was loaded on trucks or railway cars. Bessette sent two or three men to help Hippolyte during the hay-making which lasted about a month. He himself came when the job was almost finished, nearly always by the mailman's Ford or getting a lift in someone else's vehicle, for he was fearful of ruining his new Buick on the frightful, bumpy track – the very same which he described as wholly passable when it was a question of signing a petition for its improvement. The reason was simple: such an improvement would have led to an increase in his taxes. All the same, he had once journeyed in his large Buick to the shores of the Big Water Hen and had sounded his horn continuously until they came to meet him from the ranch. Hippolyte, quite independent in temper as long as Bessette was out of reach of his voice, grumbled that the merchant could bide his time, that he had no business summoning people with his klaxon while he was taking his ease on the soft front seat of his car. Nevertheless, Hippolyte had left at a good clip, followed by a handful of children who wanted at all costs to see the Buick with their own eyes. Never would they have believed that any car could be so shiny; they could see themselves in the mudguards and wherever else they looked. Impatiently Bessette had warned them off. He wanted no finger marks on his car's body; so expensive an automobile was not made to be pawed.

He passed the day at the ranch, gifted with an amazing flair for discovering anything that might be going wrong. Sometimes he was accompanied by a veterinarian, who examined the flock of sheep. Had a lamb died during the year, Hippolyte would have to describe its sickness in detail in the presence of the veterinarian, who took notes and made a diagnosis out of his textbooks. All day Hippolyte was on edge. He was a good manager, and Bessette knew it, but not for an empire would he have admitted it. He was one of those avaricious men to whom the paying of a compliment, however slight, was as painful as divesting themselves of their earthly goods. Once the flock had been inspected, he went on foot to the very end of the island to see whether the hay had been cut clean to the edges of the small poplar groves. His features betrayed nothing, neither dissatisfaction nor great annoyance. Only when he returned and saw the little school Hippolyte had built, only then did his lips open a trifle in an expression of scornful pity. He had them return him to his vehicle, and everyone was relieved to see him go. The two or three men he had hired, however, remained; often they were from the world outside, from Rorketon or from Sainte Rose du Lac. They brought news from afar. Occasionally one of them would be musically gifted, and it was pleasant of an evening to sit on the bare ground in front of the low-lying house and listen to the sound of the harmonica or the singing of cowboy songs. Luzina loved this time of year, especially once Bessette had come and gone, even though, after all, he was but one small cloud in a sky of perfect azure. Her only reservation was that all the visitors they saw from year's end to year's end came, you might say, at the same time, not giving them a real chance to savour such delights. She regretted that they could not save one visitor for the winter, when there would have been so much leisure to enjoy him to the hilt.

She had devised an ingenious signalling device so that she might be warned at least a few minutes beforehand of the Capuchin's advent. Pierre stood watch on the mainland during the third and sometimes the fourth Friday in July. The moment he recognized the missionary from afar, in the mailman's Ford, he stuck two fingers in his mouth and whistled sharply. His brother, posted on Mosquito Island, relayed the signal to yet another boy who was waiting along the banks of the Little Water Hen. Thus it was that the moment the Capuchin clambered out of Nick Sluzick's Ford, Luzina tore off her working apron, smoothed down her hair, and proceeded to the doorway.

This year Bessette had completed his inspection; no longer need they dread the embarrassment of seeing the Capuchin subjected to the merchant's digs. Even more, it was during the marvellous days of Mademoiselle Côté. Luzina was still young, in fine health and fettle. Education blazed forth from the island. One hired hand was still with them, to make a larger crowd in the house. And now on this fine summer evening, God was coming to make His annual visit. What more could you ask, truly, unless it were to wish for Heaven upon earth!

A little while after his arrival had been announced, the Capuchin appeared at the far end of the other island. Thanks to his stature, he could be descried at some distance, but the young lads who trotted through the reeds at his sides were wholly invisible. Yet already you could clearly hear their thin voices chatting with the Capuchin and coming constantly closer. He walked with the true swing of a trapper, which people said he had picked up from the halfbreeds, studying to acquire it as an external sign of his vocation. He settled himself into the small canoe, almost upsetting it with the weight of his body. His blue eyes, utterly charmed, followed the ducks in flight from their hiding-places among the reeds. The short crossing completed, he remained for a time sitting in the boat, entirely distracted by the wild purity of the spot, never suspecting that they had reached shore. Pierre laid the paddles aside and waited. At last he said, in explanation: "We've arrived home, Father."

"Why, of course! You're right, Pierre. Here we are, at home!"

Luzina was coming to greet him. She bent her chest and her knees in an odd movement which, stout as she was, threw her off balance. She cried out in her emotion, overwhelmed with reverence and the great longing her joy made obvious: "Oh! Father! You're here at last, Father! To think that you're here, Father!"

He had to bow his head when he entered the front door. He made straight for the rocking-chair, which Hippolyte immediately relinquished to him. No sooner was he installed in it than the children surrounded him; the youngest were fascinated by the whiteness of the teeth gleaming from behind the Capuchin's beard. They would have loved to touch them. They were teeth he could remove from his mouth, as had many times been proved in the past; and now, ever keen to amuse children, Father Joseph-Marie began the game they liked the best. He let the small fry examine his teeth very close; then he abruptly yanked out his denture, pretending to try to bite them. Luzina's children had never seen any other denture. Its display terrified them without, however, allaying their burning curiosity; they forgot the fearsome teeth only at the moment when the Capuchin invited them to come find for themselves, deep in his pockets, mint lozenges and lollypops. This year he had brought licorice in the shape of whips, cigars, pipes, and even tobacco pouches; the youngsters soon had lips as black as pitch. Rocking at top speed, the Capuchin then began to tell his news.

He had been able to supply the people of Rorketon with a bell, a harmonium, and the music of Handel and Bach;

those of Portage des Prés, protection against profiteers and a solemn warning against the evil effects of alcohol. In this lonely house, lacking a telephone and even a radio, he was quite satisfied to recount only local events.

"You have heard that there is something new at the Bjorgsson's?"

He had acquired the French-Canadian way of announcing births, which he considered both engaging and delicate. "The Indians stopped by their house last Tuesday night."

"You don't tell me!" said Luzina happily. This visit by the Indians the Capuchin was talking about was just the thing to interest her. Then, too, she had retained delightful memories of the Icelanders' hospitality on the occasion of her journey home in Abe Zlutkin's company, just a few years ago.

"Did the Indians leave a boy or a girl?" asked Luzina.

It was silly of him, the Capuchin had to admit, but he didn't remember. Perhaps he had not even asked. Yet as a counter-attraction, he knew by sight the fellow – a Rorketon Lithuanian – who had murdered his wife with an axe.

"With an axe!" groaned Luzina. "Father, Father! How frightful!"

He quickly shifted to a more consoling bit of news. "Our Member of Parliament has given me to understand that there might be a few loads of gravel this year to put on the road from Rorketon to Portage des Prés."

"It's on our own road that the need is greatest," remarked Hippolyte.

"True enough! True enough! ... Mrs Macfarlane is no better; her fingers are twisted completely out of shape."

"Poor woman!" Luzina commiserated with her. "Then there's nothing can be done?"

"No," sighed the old priest. "It's a tough disease."

"Are there many sicknesses like that that can't be cured?"

"Unfortunately!"

By contrast, he could report that old Connelly, who had had a cataract removed, was reading the newspaper as well as he did in his young days.

"How pleased I am!" cried Luzina, in a tone as joyful as though she had been informed of the recovery of her dearest friend.

"Medicine is making great progress," he assured them. "God is good."

"Yet there is nothing to help rheumatism?" Luzina again asked.

"Ah, no!"

He himself often suffered its pangs.

Yet this whimsicality in medical progress, to which Luzina kept drawing his attention, a thing after all somewhat unjust, since while it helped some it did nothing for others, nonetheless left him assured that that was the way things should go. God had not acted otherwise in performing His miracles.

"By the way, I shall not have my little Koussilevska for the Rorketon chapel," he informed them.

He could now laugh quietly at his aspirations. To have cast his eye on a young Ukrainian woman who had, true enough, once lived in Rorketon, but who now was well known in the capital, a featured radio singer, whose railway fare her compatriots had had to pay from Winnipeg, in short a star – he must have been losing his mind! At least it showed his good taste in music.

Ha! Ha! By an association of ideas beyond the Tousignant's ken, he joyously took up a new subject: "I have at last succeeded in marrying off my Olaf. Man is not made to live alone ... you know whom I mean, Olaf Petersen with the split ear and only one eye. . . . "

Everyone, from these characteristics, recognized the Rorketon seedsman, whom Luzina had already described to them.

"To a young Polish girl from Ochre River."

"If she took Olaf, she can't be very pretty," said Luzina.

"On the contrary, very pretty," asserted the Capuchin

who, truth to tell, found almost all women comely. "Poor Olaf! Have I ever told you how he almost died? He was then living at Winnipegosis, as a fisherman on the lake. One evening in the autumn he was far out on the water, twelve miles from shore. . . . "

They heard for the fourth time how the ice had quickly formed all round the small fishing boat and how Olaf, starting out on foot over this thin skin of ice, had lost his way. . . .

All the while Luzina was making her preparations for supper. Split between her concerns as a housekeeper and the attention she gave to what the priest was saying, she took twice as long as usual in cooking the meal, and even then she missed certain details she would have dearly loved to hear. The bother was that the Capuchin always began talking at the precise moment when she had to give her attention to fixing him a proper repast.

Suddenly he sent one of the children to fetch him his small cardboard suitcase, in which he carried, mixed among the objects he needed for his ministry, the oddest collection of things: a screwdriver, sometimes a few nuts, cream-separator parts – for he gladly undertook the errands of people who did not often go to town. He fumbled for some time in the suitcase and extracted a small metal rod and a few washers.

"Here are the parts you asked me to get for your sewing machine. I didn't forget!" The fact that he had remembered gave him the greatest satisfaction.

"How kind of you, Father!"

She examined the parts, saw that they were not at all what she had asked for, but took good care not to seem upset.

"It's nothing at all, my dear," said he, cutting short her thanks. "If you need anything else, write it down on a slip of paper. You'll have to write it down, though. I'm losing my memory."

Once again the story of Olaf had slipped from his mind. He closed his eyes. The preparation of supper, which he had so often interrupted, tickled his nostrils. So little concerned with food elsewhere, the Capuchin, when he arrived at Luzina's, was in a great hurry to draw near the table. This was the happiest stopping point on his weary round. Through his coarse woollen habit he felt the warmth of the children's bodies leaning on his shoulders or stretched against his legs. A wanderer, he felt in his limbs the fatigue of his perpetual travels, of the endless road he had covered, and the well-being of yielding to that weariness at last, for here it was that there existed for him the nearest thing to a home. Embarrassed elsewhere by the marks of respect people insisted on showing him, he liked the joyful holiday atmosphere which coincided here with his visit. He drew his chair a trifle closer.

"Father Theodulus has had three pictures painted for the Toutes Aides church," said he. "By a Hollander . . . "

"That must be beautiful, Father!"

"Hum! . . . Beautiful! . . . "

He saw again the three violently coloured murals which represented the life of the Saviour. The personages in them were clad in vermilion and bright blue; their faces were coarse. Perhaps the painter had tried to imitate the primitives; it looked amateurish. But he himself didn't know much about painting. Possibly it wasn't so bad. . . . He remembered the "Repentance of Saint Peter" by El Greco. Tears came to his eyes – tears of gratitude to an artist who had succeeded in communicating so powerful an emotion, and of pity for Saint Peter, all commingled in a joy that overcame him. That one's taste for the beautiful, for God, and for the human should thus at the same time be satisfied was almost more gratification than the heart could hold.

"It's ready. Come to the table, Father," said Luzina.

The large company took their places around him, including everyone down to the baby sitting in the high chair and already crying with desire at sight of the dishes spread before it. The cats were there, too, ready to snatch with the tips of their paws any stray piece of meat. The

Capuchin extended his plate to Luzina with the same trusting gesture as the children. Hardly had she begun to fill it when he was protesting that she had given him too much. It was true that he ate little, used to limiting his nourishment almost exclusively to doughy concoctions and cold potatoes. The only thing of which he asked a second helping was the bread. And this it was he liked best of all at Luzina's, her good homemade bread, white and so fine in texture. Each time he went into raptures, complimented her at length, and each time he asked her for the recipe, only to forget it at once, for when would he ever have time to make his own bread! He recounted, however, how he had tried once; he thought that he had done everything exactly as Luzina had told him, but what a wretched colour that bread had turned out to have!

"Not at all like this," he said with astonishment.

Perhaps he had forgotten the yeast.

Abruptly, at the end of the meal, the Capuchin stopped laughing and talking. He brushed a few crumbs from his habit. He strove to take on an air of seriousness. He arose from the table and went off alone, by himself, toward the living room near the kitchen which, during his stay with the Tousignants, served as chapel.

Before crossing its threshold, half turning toward the family, he said: "I shall be at your disposal when you wish, when it suits your convenience."

It was now the confessor who spoke to them.

VIII

Once more Luzina took off her apron, once more she smoothed her ashen hair. To give the others courage, she always went first to rejoin the priest, seated in one corner of the room, his head between his hands. She did it also to be rid the quicker of the weight of her sins. A whole year to bear their burden – it was too long, it was fearfully long!

She entered on tiptoe. The living room was in shadow;

Luzina had drawn the curtains beforehand, against the light that was too gay, too slow to disappear on these fine summer evenings, and that would not have been fitting to the gravity of the events which were to take place there. Deep in the shadows the Capuchin was seated on a small straight-backed chair. He held himself so motionless that you might have thought him asleep had you not noticed the soft, burning brilliance of his shining eyes. His shoulders were bent forward. He seemed to grow old, to lose his strength and gaiety, the moment he sat down upon this small straight chair in the darkest part of the room. A strange emotion swelled Luzina's heart. To see the missionary stooped over himself, you would have said that he was the guilty one and that he was as though bowed down under the weight of evil.

Luzina knelt upon the floor almost at the Capuchin's feet.

"Father! ... " she began and, at a loss, hesitated a long while.

He had glanced away so as not to frighten her, but when she thus uttered the word "Father ... " he was constrained to bring his eyes back toward her, exactly like a father whom his daughter calls.

Curious was his feeling with regard to this woman, perhaps with regard to all women, yet no, with regard to this one especially. As was fitting for a reply to that cry of "Father," the affection he experienced was pure and deep. Without a family, without children, without a wife, the Capuchin felt vibrant within him a nostalgia for fatherhood. An inclination came to him to stretch out his hand, to touch Luzina's fresh cheek with the tips of his fingers, in a father's furtive caress of his child. Yet to this paternal emotion was added man's old hunger to be coddled, fondled, protected by a woman's wholly motherly affection. And it was at once to his daughter and to the woman's protective soul that he spoke: "Yes, my child!"

She began by confessing her trivial faults of impatience with the children; then she came to her duties as a wife.

Each year in the same place Luzina blushingly confided to the Capuchin that she did not yield with entire submission to the demands of the married state. She had not the words to express delicately what it was already so hard for her to admit at all. She would have wished the babies to come at somewhat longer intervals. She was at first ill-tempered, inclined to becoming discouraged, she said, when she discovered that she was again "in a family way." She summed up the situation: "Understand, Father, the children I already have I would not exchange for all the gold in the world, but I should almost like it better not to have so many. It's wrong to think that way, isn't it, Father?"

Now the missionary, each time, found it difficult not to get angry: "What are you telling me, my daughter! You have had ten children in fourteen years of marriage. See here! Don't talk to me about sins. It is sinful to judge our Father Who sees better than you do yourself into your own heart."

"But I take it badly," Luzina accused herself. "I kick over the traces,"

He stealthily cast a penetrating, saddened glance at her. Even in the confessional it was not the bad side of human nature which struck him. There he very often understood the good will of souls. Sometimes the revelation of this rectitude struck him to the heart. Then he would look beyond his penitent, his eyes filled with melancholy, and what he contemplated was the inexhaustible sum of goodness on earth, the tragic, perfect good will of so many human beings, which all the same did not succeed in changing the world. "Come, now; don't say foolish things!"

His mind's eye abruptly focused on a most odd experience in his life. It was in March. A violent windstorm had taken him by surprise on the shores of Lake Winnipegosis. There, more than in any other part of the lake country, the wind blew strong. He had found asylum in a small dwelling exposed like a lighthouse to the whirling snow and the crashing waves. Night was falling. It turned out that his hosts were Finns, very poor people such as there are in that region, who lived wholly from fishing. The young woman had come to kiss his hand at the door sill, saying that God Himself, in response to her appeal, had sent the missionary. Her time had come; Pietr, her husband, hesitated to go for help. How could he succeed in getting any? The telephone was four miles away. Supposing he should reach it, surely the midwife herself would not be able to travel in such weather. Pietr was moaning, his head clasped in his hands. Why had he ever settled in this cruel country? What could he have been thinking about when he brought a woman there? At last he made up his mind to go, just as the Capuchin began to affix his own snow shoes.

He had spent the whole night alone with Christina. Pietr must have lost his way or, half frozen, stopped along the road at some neighbour's house. Then, too, the midwife might be on a call at the other end of the country. He had imagined himself in Christina's place, alone with the strange companion that he was, and he had understood Christina's loneliness to be that of no other human being. She might be as old as nineteen. It was her first child. Suddenly she called her mother, her mother who was somewhere in Finland. Anguish reigned in the tiny house buffeted by the wind. Had he ever experienced anguish before this night! He reproached himself for not having himself gone to seek aid. What was the cause of his anguish? What was taking place before his eyes was the most normal event of our human state. At last day broke. Pietr still had not returned. The Capuchin had made some coffee for Christina; he had forced her to drink it. And he walked. He strode up and down across the room. Only something very ordinary was taking place there, a birth among a thousand million others, and yet he felt sweat dripping from him, and his hands shook. What he was to remember longest was to how great a degree Christina had seemed to him little made for suffering, fashioned as though to escape it by a divine intention of beauty, of daintiness.

He had had to assist her. It was he himself who had bathed the child and wrapped it in a blanket. When Pietr had returned accompanied by the midwife, Father Joseph-Marie, standing on the threshold, had motioned to them not to disturb Christina. She was asleep. The house was clean. He had had time to sweep, to build up the fire, and to set fresh coffee to boil. He had been at peace in his soul since the moment when he had brought close to Christina the little infant which he had forced to take its first breath, had warmed, and had swathed in its coverings. The world's pain remained inviolate for him, always inexplicable; but the same held true for joy and love.

"My penance? You haven't given me any penance," said Luzina.

"Your penance! Three Hail Marys and one Our Father, my daughter."

She arose. She went away with her heart light. He called her back in a humble, almost piteous voice. "My daughter, I tore my habit again while coming across the little island. Could you patch it up a bit for me?"

She whispered: "Hang your habit on your doorknob; I'll get it when you have gone to bed."

Shortly Hippolyte took his turn, abashed, his eyes downcast.

The Capuchin was waiting for the wretch. Ten children in fourteen years of married life, and not yet satisfied!

But his wrath quickly melted away. A little ashamed, a little astonished, Hippolyte listened to an odd sermon, a sort of tender plea on behalf of "creatures"; for according to French-Canadian custom, the Capuchin used this term, which he thought altogether polite, in referring to women. Creatures, said he, were of a weak constitution, their "mechanism" was delicate. They needed consideration. Creatures were not made to satisfy men's untrammelled passions or to reproduce the human race without stop and periods of rest. A good husband took into account his wife's health, the difficulties of the life she led. The Capuchin cited Saint Joseph, Mary's chaste spouse. He cited Saint Joachim, the husband of Saint Anne, who, according to Scripture, seemed to have had only the Blessed Virgin by her. He mentioned the names of many celibates who had been canonized by the Church. He was surprised at the small number of fathers of large families to be found among the saints. He was even somewhat at a loss. Seek as he might, he did not know of a single one. All this, moreover, remained basically somewhat strange. After having implanted the carnal love which was indispensable to His designs, God seemed nonetheless to prefer those who abstained from it. Hence had everyone wanted to be perfect, the earth would long ago have become depopulated. How curious. The Capuchin thought that he would like to examine the problem at leisure one of these days, but truth to tell, this would probably be another riddle he would have to leave to the Lord.

He lowered his eyes toward Hippolyte in a glance full of compassion. It seemed to him that it was perhaps Hippolyte, after all, who stood in greatest need of it.

He took some time in getting to sleep, stretched out on the sofa in the living room. At the very end of the room a small altar had already been set up by the efforts of Luzina and the schoolmistress, yet for the time being it was still necessary to use the living room as a bedroom. To the missionary, accustomed to otherwise rugged sleeping accommodations, the sofa seemed most comfortable. Nor was it the fact of being in a strange bed that disturbed him. He never slept very long in the same place, and he had acquired a wonderful facility in adapting himself to the various spots where he stopped along the road. He found it no more singular, this evening, to be in bed in Luzina's house than he would be astonished the day after tomorrow to lie on the ground under a tent near the Indian reservation. Luzina's comings and goings – she had to use the living room as a passageway since all the others opened off it – did not annoy him in the least. She crept through quietly, from her own bedchamber to the kitchen. She slipped through, her shoulders hunched as though the better to pass unnoticed. She needed her sewing basket, left behind in her own room, or else to get some article of clothing she wanted to brush and make ready for the morrow. As she herself put it, she tried "to have everything out beforehand," but rarely did she succeed in foreseeing all. She had excused herself for thus having "to cross through your room, Father. . . . My clothes closet is the other side, as well as my best clothes, which I keep there away from the dust. . . . " He had begged her not to worry about him, assuring her that he slept like an old log, that nothing could keep him from slipping off to sleep the moment his head touched the pillow. Truly a whopping lie, for he had continued in so acute a state of emotional receptiveness and nervous excitability that from every trifling incident he drew matter for sharp pain or joy. Not far from him, on another sofa pushed against the partition opposite, two of Luzina's little boys lay asleep. The children's movements, their breathing, he believed did not disturb him. But what a lot of trouble he had given once again in this small house! He should have insisted on sleeping outdoors, under the trees. It would not have been the first time.

Moreover, you might say the sofa was too comfortable, equipped with springs just like a hotel bed. Luzina had provided him with a big feather pillow, too large and soft. She had slipped it into a fresh pillowcase and given him clean sheets, and he considered this wasteful, since he was going to be there only for a single night. What he thoroughly appreciated was the pure fresh air from the river, which he breathed through the open window. It pleased him also to hear the calling of the birds that from time to time pierced the deep night. How happy he was in this home of Luzina's! The very excess of his well-being prevented his taking his rest. Lying flat on his back, his eyes wide open, happiness seemed to him that night so easy, so very easy, that he grieved not to be able to make the whole world understand it. What more was it, indeed, than to trust yourself entirely to God! Not to worry about the morrow!

At this instant Luzina again half opened the door and crossed the room almost stealthily. Why wasn't she asleep yet, the Capuchin asked himself, at so late an hour? He had utterly forgot that he had asked her to repair his habit. So it seemed to him that she did not rely enough upon God, who had never asked more than the small daily effort of which each of us is capable. Tomorrow he would speak to her about it. "Verily I say unto you, Solomon in all his glory was not clad as one of these. . . . " He would have to remind Luzina of that lesson. Explain to her that God had never required a person to stay up until after midnight. Whereupon he at last went peacefully to sleep, his soul quiet, while Luzina spread out on the kitchen table the Capuchin's poor habit, and studying it carefully, appraised the damage and the best way to mend it. The tear was quite serious, and the cloth all round it was worn very thin into the bargain. At once Luzina decided that it would be absolutely necessary to apply a patch. To arrange matters so that it would not be too obvious – there was the problem. Hence it had been to rummage in her scrapbag that she had once again disturbed the "poor Father," who slept like an old man, very badly, whatever he might claim. Dear old man! Dear soul, simple and tender! To have him under her roof, so trusting, so undemanding, gave Luzina the impression of having one more child in her care.

Still, what a tear! To do a decent job would take an hour or two. It was time the Capuchin bought himself a new habit. Surely no one took any care of him, kept him a bit in order.

If after many eliminations and simplifications the Capuchin had at last achieved an altogether intimate, altogether familiar image of God, how much more directly yet did Luzina arrive at it that evening, thanks to the worn old habit impregnated with the smell of tobacco! God must be of the very same kind as the Capuchin, knowing almost all languages, a great Latin scholar, a mighty traveller who had seen everything, now aged and doubtless tired, yet, precisely because he was beyond petty things, little skilled at dealing with them.

Come to think of it, what a fix God would be in, Luzina tenderly reflected, if we did not do the bulk of the practical things on earth! If we didn't get married! If we had no children! If we were no longer willing to mend and cook the meals!

A surge of wholly motherly affection toward God overwhelmed Luzina. In coming to the Little Water Hen, where there was only one house in which to take refuge, had not God entrusted Himself to her, the only woman on the island! Her goodness of will increased tenfold. She would take advantage of her stove's still being hot to set her heavy wooden-handled irons upon it. She would dampen the habit and press it, put it outside an hour or two, in the night's broad air, which would give it a good clean smell of wind. But she must not forget to pluck her chickens, to draw them beforehand, if she wanted to have everything ready for the breakfast she gave after the mission was over.

Starting some years earlier, this breakfast had become an institution. From the beginning she could not resign herself to seeing the neighbours leave without offering them something to eat when they had come such great distances fasting; then from year to year she had made her reception more and more of an event. And her heart had grown attached to this small feast which, without her understanding it fully, made beautiful her house as, in an earlier day, the brotherly love-feasts had done among the first Christians.

So she went to bed very late and got up not long afterward. Wholly clothed, she crossed the living room, but now, just as she was leaving it, standing at a respectful distance from the Capuchin who was still asleep, she cried: "Father! Father! It is almost six o'clock. The Sluzicks are arriving, Father. Everybody will soon be here, Father!"

Then she went to knock on the doors of the two bedrooms and enjoined those who were sleeping there: "Father is getting up. Wait a few minutes before you leave your rooms."

IX

A regular small crowd of people in their Sunday best now occupied the living room, which no longer gave the least hint of having served as dormitory. In the front row could be seen the Sluzick family, to whom Luzina always gave the position of honour, seated on the best kitchen chairs, lined up as though they were in church. You could also see the Joe Mackenzies, who at that period lived in their Partridge Point cabin, five miles to the west, and to whom Luzina had sent a messenger the day before, announcing: "The Capuchin will say Mass at our house tomorrow."

On his own account, Nick Sluzick had informed two unmarried trappers, one of whom was called Tom Mackenzie and the other a Frenchman living on Lake Water Hen, a chap name Perrochon or Rochon or Peisson, no one was quite sure which. Having left his own small house ten miles to the north very early, almost in darkness, Nick had picked both of them up along the trail and brought them in his Ford, already full to overflowing. Then came the Tousignant family complete, among them the hired man and their schoolteacher. Mademoiselle Côté had come to the chapel from her adjoining room wearing a hat; it was that famous hat with the red feather which had made so great an impression the day of her arrival. Luzina, having no veil to her name either, had followed the teacher's example and was wearing the hat reserved for great happenings. Since she donned this velvet bonnet but once a year for the trip to Sainte Rose du Lac, she felt very strange wearing it in her own house without any other place to go. From time to time she had to leave the church a moment to cast a glance at her chickens in the oven, at the baby left behind in the kitchen and, whenever she went near the stove, she was quite nonplussed to catch a glimpse of her strange outfit, her cotton dress and her town hat reflected on the enamelled surface of the dish warmer. Despite the solemnity of the day, she had an embarrassed little half-smile each time she returned to kneel with the others on the living room floor and bent her hat piously forward.

The congregation sat down to listen to the sermon. They almost completely filled the room, from the back end, where the two sofas placed side by side made a long pew for the use of the faithful, to the front, where they crowded the altar – a small table covered with a spotless cloth and adorned by the schoolteacher with wild flowers: tiger lilies, pink and white bramble roses, and field daisies. Hence the priest had only to turn round to find himself in his pulpit; a step forward and he would have been amongst the faithful, a step backward and he would have jostled the altar. To some slight extent he envied priests who can address their people from afar, from above, and under the shelter of a sounding board. A raised pulpit, distance, and perhaps even those loudspeakers installed in certain churches must give preachers real self-possession. Though it surely would be frightening to find oneself so open to the public gaze! Lower down, however, it was just as bad. Placed thus on the same level as the faithful, you could not try to overawe them. A man among other men, very little cleverer than they – that's what you had to remember!

The Capuchin slipped his hands into his sleeves and asked himself what on earth he was going to talk about. Sometimes he prepared his sermons in advance. Yet, apart from the fact that his memory served him ill, it had often happened that at the moment of opening his mouth he had of a sudden preferred to the planned subject, already elaborated in his mind, some other which seemed more fitting. Occasionally circumstances led him to such a shift. Thus once, when he was going to speak on the infallibility of the Pope, he had spotted Mrs Macfarlane in the congregation, who from time to time came to his sermons. He had immediately realized to what an extent he might have seemed to be aiming directly at this person, who not only was sincere in her convictions but also happened to be the donor of the harmonium. It was not as though he would have to forgo forever dealing with the Pope's infallibility. Yet since there were so many subjects which drew people together, why not choose one of them? In this fashion, little by little, and without being much aware of it himself, the Capuchin had come to one sole subject, and it was substantially always the same subject which, were it at Rorketon or at Portage des Prés, were it for the Tousignants or for the halfbreeds, he in the end elaborated, each time thinking that he had found something new. True enough, being thoroughly versed in it, the Capuchin, like some virtuoso who has long played the same instrument, was constantly able to adorn it with unexpected variations. This aged man preached of love, which he would preach from one end of the lake country to the other, and all things served to make it fresh, to keep it living. Motherly devotion, as manifest in the tender care of animals for their young, family relationships, nature, the forest, the trees, the flowers, and the bees – all were put to use.

Now, as he stood there, almost mingling with the faithful, it occurred to him that love blazed forth from the lives of the native birds; he had been struck by it the evening before when, drawing apart to say his prayers, he had watched a prairie chickens' ball. A first hen, fat and strutting, had marched into a small clearing; she had summoned others with the forceful drumming of her wings. Then several couples had appeared. They had taken the formation of a proper quadrille, and each dancer had solemnly described a figure seven, without taking his

round eyes off his partner, a brilliant image of courtesy
and fine manners. The figures seemed very strictly pat-
terned, like those in a ballet. Each performer went
through this figure seven once, and then again and, passing before his partner, I bow to you, you bow to me, I
ruffle my plumage and you do the same. Exactly like
human beings. It was the formal ball preceding their pair-
ing off under the branches, a presentation ball, if you like,
at which, under court etiquette, the cocks, like great lords,
politely signified their intentions to the ladies with their
puffed-out feathers. It had pleased the Capuchin to see
here an astonishing manifestation of the love infused by
God in His creation. He began his sermon. And this is
approximately what they heard – the two old trappers,
Mrs Mackenzie, busy dandling her baby in her arms,
whom she thus hoped to distract from its hunger, in short,
the entire, most attentive, though slightly astonished,
group:

Souls, said the Capuchin, were a little like the birds.
Some were heavy and could barely fly. You have all seen
prairie chickens? he asked and, at the slight nods of assent
registered especially by the women and children, the Capuchin pointed out that these birds did not go very high,
that they just succeeded in leaving the ground. Nonetheless, they made their small effort, and thus was it with
many souls; they tried to soar on high, they tried to know
Heaven, but they were held back by their earthly concerns
and their passions, and they soon tumbled back to earth.
You must be more daring and perseverant if you wished
to attain a certain height. He then turned to the water
hens. Here were birds already much lighter. Had you seen
them soar up, perfectly skilled in the air? Yes, Luzina's
children had often seen this sight, this superiority of the
water hens over the poor prairie chickens, and they
showed it by their shining eyes and their complete agree-
ment. And the wild ducks! continued the priest. They too
had light wings. So likewise the bitterns, the herons, the
loons, the various waders, all of which, large and clumsy

when they were on land, seemed not a bit heavy when they were in full flight. ... Have you ever noticed, asked the Capuchin, who seemed to be addressing his question especially to Nick Sluzick, how these birds, not very elegant when seen close by, present gracious lines when immersed in their proper element? ... Nick seemed to be considering the matter with annoyance, very ill will and, to tell the truth, with helpless amazement. ... Souls created by God for the purity and the light of Heaven in like manner achieved their real element only when, by a great effort, they had wrenched themselves free from the slime, the mud, the "gumbo" of human passions.

Abruptly Father Joseph-Marie ceased speaking French; he launched out in the Ukrainian tongue, whereupon Mrs Sluzick, enraptured at understanding at last what was going on, gave her approval with a sweet smile spread all across her face. The French-speaking parishioners, however, had assumed a somewhat vexed expression, disappointed at being thus abandoned when things were becoming so especially interesting. What was the Capuchin talking about now? No one of them could refrain from trying to guess the answer by watching the faces of the Ukrainians. Yet it seemed that Mrs Sluzick's face was more and more radiant, while Nick Sluzick's contracted more and more into a frown. A brilliantly white kerchief enveloped the Ukrainian woman's head and gave her features a soft brilliance; it was a typically Slavic countenance, with very prominent cheekbones and an often sorrowful expression. The dark eyes burned with pain long borne in silence. Everyone knew that Nick Sluzick, jealous and suspicious, held her in genuine durance in the remotest part of the region, near the Indian reservation, where they dwelt ten miles from the nearest white family. The mission was the only occasion when Nick Sluzick allowed the poor woman to be seen – to such an extent that she had to await this reunion in full summer to distribute at Luzina's the handsome tinted Easter eggs which she had kept – wasn't it thoughtful of her? – all that length of time for the benefit of the Tousignants. Naturally the eggs were no longer edible, but they still were adorned with their charming designs in their vivid colours. Martha Sluzick would have liked to have done much more. Generous by nature, she felt humiliated at having so often accepted Luzina's hospitality without hope of ever returning it in kind. And since she had not been able to learn French, she suffered even more at being unable to explain herself in this matter, thus perhaps leaving Luzina under the impression that she did not appreciate her kindness. This was certainly the reason her eyes had become so expressive, as though deputized to unburden her heart of all the things that weighed upon it, and very often they succeeded in both smiling and weeping at the same time.

The Capuchin was well aware of old Nick's unsociableness and of the sad lot that was Martha's. There is only one brief step between birds and freedom, and so it was of freedom that he spoke, always in Ukrainian, and mainly inspired by Martha's lovely, shadowed glance, which seemed to thank him for the mere fact of being understood.

Like the birds, said he, the human soul had need of air, of freedom, and of its fellows. In a cage it could only pine away. With its wretched wings it beat at the bars, wore itself out in trying to rejoin its comrades in freedom.... He hoped Nick had understood. He seemed to have, judging by the deeper and deeper frown on his face, but in case he had not fully grasped the similitude, the Capuchin added that certain husbands presumed to hold their wives as neither more nor less than prisoners, that this ran counter to the joys permitted women and hence was displeasing to God. Jesus had liked social gatherings; He had honoured them with His presence. Jesus had attended the marriage at Cana. He was certain that He would tolerate, that He would approve seemly rejoicing.

Nick's young daughters, Maria, Olga, and Irina, appeared to be delighted with the sermon and hoped that the Capuchin would say enough to oblige their father to let them dance that evening at the halfbreeds' festival. Meanwhile the aged mailman stared at his shoes with an air of fury. According to Nick, everyone should attend to his own business, the good Lord to His, and he, Sluzick, to his wife and daughters, whom he was not going to let run loose. A Catholic according to the Greek Rite, Nick was not at all certain that what he heard here were God's true words and specific commandments. There was no icon, no Slavonic chant. The priest who had married him in his Carpathian village had himself had a wife and children, and he was not one to give women too much freedom; that fellow knew how things stood. The Capuchin, without encumbrances of this sort, could prate at his ease of freedom, of rejoicing, and of birds. He ran no risk. Besides, Nick had brought his whole family to the mission; that was enough entertainment for a year. And if they kept goading him, bothering him, it would be within his power to load up all his people immediately after Mass instead of letting the women jabber almost the whole day long, as they had in preceding years. After all, that was the way it went with women; you gave them an arm's length of freedom, and at once they wanted to go gadding, a train trip next time, God knows what at the end of a few years! Beside the mailman sat fourteen-year-old Sluzick junior. His arms were crossed on his chest, and he looked almost as sullen as his father.

Happily the Capuchin went back to his birds and to the French language. They thought it wonderful that, returning from so long a digression, he could continue from exactly the point where he had left off ten minutes earlier. Certain souls, then, flew much higher than others. This was the case with the smaller birds, warblers, swallows, woodpeckers, lithesome creatures who ever better and better soared to great heights. It was the lark, though, which certainly climbed the highest in the heavens.

"Have you ever seen it, so slender?" inquired the good priest, a trifle exalted, his eyes smiling at the picture he saw so clearly of a tiny bird. "Brave little creature," said he, "flying up and up, to utter there aloft, so far away, its cry of joy and of love?"

At this moment, however, Luzina, especially entranced by the example of the lark, thought she heard from the kitchen a sound of violent boiling and the rattle of a saucepan cover. She had to rush off to see what was happening on the stove. When she came tiptoeing back, she slowed her pace as she crossed the threshold of the church. She had suddenly been struck by a sorrowful idea. The kitchen, her baby, cooking the meals, a hundred distractions prevented her from perfectly approaching God. It might well be that she was of the heavy kind about which the Capuchin had spoken, held down from flight by earthly things. Perhaps she was only in the prairie chicken class, very heavy and very clumsy. She did look like them, she thought, with her often swollen legs and her plump chest. At that moment almost all the rest of the faithful were likewise preoccupied in determining which species they most closely resembled, but even more in what category to place their neighbours. As for Hippolyte, the first problem did not bother him at all; he could not in any way imagine himself as a bird; and yet he had not had the slightest hesitation in placing Bessette among the crows and hawks. Whereas the halfbreeds, with their rich imaginations, all recognized themselves in the graceful lark. Such were the Capuchin's birds; they did not spin or weave or garner into barns or worry much about the future; and consider divine justice! It was always they who would be the best clad! Solomon in all his glory would never be as beautiful as any one of them.

Now the Capuchin gave a summary of his sermon in English, for the benefit of Tom Mackenzie, who had only a smattering of French. Every man, according to Father Joseph-Marie, had the right to hear God talked about in his own language. Moreover, he had something for which to reproach Tom Mackenzie in particular. At first sight Tom Mackenzie seemed the most sociable being one could imagine, a fine old hunter with greying hair, his eyes smiling, his mouth smiling, even his sensitive, attentive ears seemed to share in his broad smile. His costume amply proclaimed Tom's regard for civilization. It was made up of garments such as never had been seen assembled on one man's body, save the trapper's. Around his legs were wrapped khaki puttees of the sort worn by soldiers in the 1914 war. His jacket of blue serge with gilded buttons was that of a railwayman. As for Tom's hat, at that moment resting on his knees, a wide, light tan hat of hard felt, something like a Boy Scout's, with a band running round the nape of the neck, it was assuredly straight out of the Mounted Police. Halfbreeds have a very marked liking for uniforms, and they usually succeed in assembling themselves some outfit resembling a uniform by means of barter. Had Tom in his travels encountered a conductor, a soldier, and a Mounted Policeman who had each yielded him a part of what constituted their splendour in the old halfbreed's eyes? Perhaps, more prosaically, he had found the whole outfit in those bales of clothing which certain charitable organizations assembled from what had been given them by the widest variety of donors and then shipped, in poverty-stricken years, to the lost regions. Whatever its origin, Tom wore his collection for Sunday best without the least embarrassment; on the contrary, with a profound sense of well-being. Despite all this, this eminently friendly soul, this kindly Tom, had a still, and brewed in his cabin a wretched, very potent beverage, to which he generously treated his friends, passers-by, and the world in general.

Greatly interested, the old trapper listened to the Capuchin talk of eagles, hawks, and owls, evil birds, birds of prey, which did great harm to husbandry and brought terror to defenceless smaller birds. Such was alcohol, said the Capuchin, an enemy that treacherously undermined, corrupted, and destroyed. Neither Tom, with his every smiling face, nor Hippolyte, who more than ever saw Bessette as a crow, nor even the good Capuchin bethought themselves that these cruel birds, especially the hawk, flew very high, at least as high as the tiny lark which rose to the roof of Heaven to utter its cry of love.

The odours of the feast spilled over from the kitchen, more and more mouth-watering. Mrs Joe Mackenzie in vain bounced her baby as hard as she was able; no longer could she distract it from howling. A kitten came to the chapel doorway to see what was so long retaining the people of the house. Luzina's children, horrified, tried to drive it away. "Go way, kitty . . . ," they whispered. Then, abruptly, almost without transition, the Capuchin let drop his "Amen. That is the grace which I wish you with all my heart, as I bless you."

Five minutes later the room had again changed atmosphere and intention. The big kitchen table had been brought in and chairs had been ranged around it; dishes of food were making their appearance; meanwhile Nick Sluzick, bored by all this ceremoniousness, was the first to sit down, at the place he had occupied the year before; Luzina rushed around, out of breath; the cats mewed; the schoolmistress helped; and the halfbreeds, excited by the festive air, were already tendering invitations to their own feast, which would be given that very evening and which would continue for several days.

"You'll come to our dance, 'Tigneur!" they kept begging the Capuchin.

Certainly he'd be there. After religious emotion, what more agreeable than social joy, happy faces around him, friendship in every glance!

X

The dance took place in the open air, on a small platform of planks erected among a few dwarf poplars and birches, several miles from Luzina's in the direction of the trapper Tom Mackenzie's abode. He it was who led the dance, his Royal Mounted Police hat shoved back on his head, his fiddle under his chin, his soldier's legs crossed one over the other, his buttons inscribed with the name of the national railway twinkling, and giving despite all this – what was far more extraordinary – the appearance of being entirely himself, with his handsome, almost white hair hanging down over his neck, his high cheekbones, his Indian heritage of naturalness.

The lighting was ingenious: it was furnished by three lanterns tied to the branches of the trees surrounding the platform, but so well hidden was it in the greenery that the glow seemed to come from the glossy, trembling leaves of the small poplars themselves. This unusual illumination drew mosquitoes from the whole neighbourhood. They whirled with the dancers, thirsting for blood; they buzzed so loud in your hair and ears that you almost heard them better than the trapper-violinist's "Red River Reel."

It was a very hot night, moist, nearly without a breath of wind. The party in progress so far from any dwelling might greatly have astonished a stranger who happened to hear its clamour across the flat swampland. But there was nothing surprising about it in the eyes of the halfbreeds who liked in this fashion to satisfy their very lively and contradictory tastes for solitude and sociability.

Their black hair was plastered against their foreheads and their cheeks, so hard did they work at dancing and slapping mosquitoes. At any moment you could see a dancer let go his partner's waist, clap himself sharply on the cheek, the back, or the neck, then briskly dance off again with his companion. Considerately they did each other the service of killing each other's mosquitoes. A smudge, indeed, had been made in an old bucket punched with holes, and it even wafted its choking stench over everyone at those moments when a tiny breeze drove its smoke toward the platform, but when the air moved in the opposite direction, the mosquitoes resumed their attack. Thus you suffered two miseries: either the smoke which caught in your throat, or the insects. The Capuchin in his thick woollen habit and his heavy ribbed stockings, which he wore at all seasons, with the further protection of his beard, appeared to suffer the least.

He was sitting, his legs spread apart and his back against a tree trunk, on a heavy plank arranged at the edge of the platform for the benefit of the guests of honour. Beside him sat Luzina, then Albert Patenaude, the hired man, and Mademoiselle Côté, whom the hired man was courting shamelessly. The schoolmistress's presence impressed the various Mackenzies even more, perhaps, than did that of the Capuchin. Never had there been seen at their celebration a young city girl, so composedly seated on her plank, her two feet side by side in front of her and her little handbag on her knees. The halfbreeds had been so keenly flattered by her presence that at the outset of the festivities they had put their heads together to decide on the best means of greeting her officially. They had finally persuaded Tom Mackenzie, with a shove or two in the back, to fulfil this duty. Tom was not used to speaking in public. Yet everyone agreed he had done a very good job of it. "We have with us tonight a young city lady," Tom had recited, looking down from the small platform, "a young lady with diploma, *maîtresse d'école*, schoolteacher in both languages, bilingual and what have you: Miss Côté. It is a great honour, and I'll ask every one of you to behave, on account of this little lady from Sainte Agathe, Manitoba, very nice lady, and come now, begin the dance. Ask your lady, form your company. . . . "

There were some forty of them, grown-ups and children, come from all directions and from the farthest outposts in the land. The Frenchman, Perrochon or Peisson or Rochon, was there, a silent man who did not seem particularly affable. The greater part of them were from Portage des Prés and eager for a good time. All had come as best they might, bulging the bodies of the two ancient automobiles requisitioned for the occasion. Samson had brought eleven people in his five-passenger car. Having deposited them at the party, he had at once left to get others, just exactly like election time, when he was hired to bring in the voters. One couple had made the trip bareback on the same mount, a handsome dappled horse. This vigorous steed, for the time being attached by the bridle to one of the small poplars from which a lantern was hung, shook the whole lighting system when he stretched his head to reach the small toothsome leaves. The two Fords parked amid the wild oats, a small tent pitched some distance away in which women were preparing coffee, the brightly illuminated little platform trembling under the dancers' weighty tread, the horse which was almost one of the guests – all this gave the halfbreeds' party a brilliant and particularly successful look. The Capuchin had heard bad reports of these rustic balls in the Water Hen country; according to certain Oblates who served the Indian reservation, such dancing parties served as excuse for drinking bouts, each participant bringing his own bottle of whiskey; at any moment you might see couples wandering off into the thickets.

The Capuchin saw nothing as serious as all that. True, from time to time, two or three Mackenzies and Parisiens disappeared. When they returned, the missionary believed he recognized, mingled with the perfume of clover and the night, a somewhat acrid odour, which might well be that of alcohol. But they were all standing perfectly straight on their feet when they came back from their expeditions behind the tent, and these trips, moreover, were never of long duration. Apparently it embarrassed them more than was usually the case when they gave their guests of honour the slip. They certainly were making an effort not to drink too often or too much at a time. In any case, no woman disappeared with the men into the shadows. The women remained full in the light, and that was always something gained. It was even a great deal gained when you considered how hot-blooded were these lovely girls with their elongated, flashing eyes. Surely God required no more. The Capuchin recalled the gracious ball of the prairie chickens, and it seemed to him that his halfbreeds were behaving in about the same natural way desired by the

Creator. After the pains they had all taken to have a little pleasure, the heat, the mosquito-hunting, the fact of having so bestirred themselves on so sultry a night seemed to the Capuchin more like a penance.

His worry for fear he might see people demean themselves badly therefore evaporated altogether. Soon Tom Mackenzie's unpretentious music led even him to beat time with the bottom of his coarse boots. They were old Scottish airs which the violin player mingled according to his fancy. While he played, he called the figures of the square dance:

"Gentlemen and ladies next ... on the right hand ... on the left hand ... promenade around the place ... all around the place ... Swing!"

An access of mad gaiety at that moment spurred everyone on.

"Gentlemen and ladies bow," commanded Tom Mackenzie.

He was seated on a log, as though it were a throne, his upper body very straight, almost motionless. The only part of him that moved was the arm that pushed the bow, and the whole while Tom's rigid eyes gave the impression of looking at least ten miles off into the distance. Yet nothing escaped his attention, and he knew when it was appropriate to invite the dancers to wheel, to cross hands, to bow.

Even Luzina was having a go at it this time. She had needed a lot of urging, protesting that she was rusty, that her dancing days were over, that it was not fitting that she, the mother of a family, should start hopping up and down, that in any case she would not know how to go about it, but all this with an obvious eagerness to accept. And now her face, resting against Hippolyte's shoulder, shone with pleasure. You could see that she must have been rather pretty; an ash blonde with blue eyes and a clear complexion. Her waist was a trifle heavy, her arms overplump, but she gave every sign at that moment, her eyes lifted toward Hippolyte, of seeing him as he had been in the days of their betrothal, and the expression on her face was one of renewed youth, almost of teasing. He had become a stout, thickset little man, his shoulders too brawny, nearly without a neck, yet he must also have been remembering the days of their young love, for he feared less than usual to show himself attentive to her in public. The Capuchin watched them tenderly. He thoroughly approved of that conjugal love which is accompanied by joy, by lightheartedness and, it must be added, by frank and honest desire.

Soon there remained but three persons sitting on the small platform: the Capuchin beside Mademoiselle Côté, and opposite them the Frenchman. With his twinkling eyes and a slight movement of his head, Father Joseph-Marie certainly looked as though he were urging them to dance together. Was it the priest's invitation that finally broke down the bachelor's reticence? He came and bowed low to Mademoiselle Côté, saluting her after a fashion which had never before been seen in the Little Water Hen country. She arose blushing, pleased at the Frenchman's behaviour. All around, the halfbreeds applauded. They had feared to make themselves ridiculous by asking this Miss Côté from the South, with her schoolteacher's diploma in the two languages, to dance. But to their minds, the same thing did not at all apply to the Frenchman. If anyone could be suitable for Miss Côté, it was surely the representative of France among them, the country above all others for ceremonious greetings, gallantry, and everything they involved. So they felt very proud to have him on hand for this gala occasion. Tom, out of regard for the Frenchman's beautiful native land, even tried to give a Gallic feeling to his monotonous old jigs.

As a matter of fact, Tom loved all countries, at least those the names of which were known to him – Spain, Greece, Italy, the Vatican, and the United States. Tom loved countries as he innocently loved uniforms, soldiers, aeroplanes. But his liking for civilization had come to Tom through Scotland, as had his flowers of speech, his pretty compliments. This was doubtless why his jigging seemed less natural when he began to drone it out in French.

"*Les mesdames et les monsieurs . . . ,*" chanted Tom, "*la madame* on the left . . . *le monsieur* on the right . . . *croisez les mains . . . la belle dame . . . le monsieur . . .*"

The awkwardness of his speech touched the priest's heart.

Above his old head shone billions of bright stars; in the grass fireflies emitted their brief sparks of light.

Upon the tips of the high-standing grasses, when they bent in the lantern glow, great flowers took shape, only to melt away a moment later.

The Capuchin crossed his heavy boots, with their eyelets and tiny hooks. He drew his pipe out of his pocket. He lit it, less because he wanted to smoke than to give the mosquitoes a bit more opposition. Deep within the bluish haze, his eyes sparkled.

To him also the old civilization seemed faraway, lovable, gracious.

The farther he had gone into the North, the more he had been free to love.

Afterword

BY SANDRA BIRDSELL

IN THE OPENING paragraphs of *Where Nests the Water Hen*, Gabrielle Roy takes us by the hand and leads us down into the flat, broad landscape of Manitoba. With graceful and poetic prose, she draws us into the north country of Manitoba, that sparsely populated land of water and grass, to the tiny outpost of Portage des Prés. We are persuaded to walk quietly along a barely discernible path to the edge of a river and to listen, "wholly wrapped in such silence as is seldom found on earth," to that sound of silence as we cross the water of the Little and Big Hen rivers. When we reach a large island inhabited by sheep and the Tousignant family, we have already entered the dream of an idyllic, fairy-tale world where the people appear foreign or from another century, a broad place where the profound silence is accentuated by the sound of wind in grass and the cries of the ever-present water hen mingling with the cries of children. In this landscape time is like sky meeting water, egg-shaped, elliptical. As we read, we become children and the joy, unity, and peace of Luzina Tousignant's world where "tenderness and anxiety are one" become real.

Gabrielle Roy began writing *Where Nests the Water Hen* in 1947 when she was living in France. Ten years earlier she had taught school in the Little Water Hen district. In her autobiography, *Enchantment and Sorrow*, she recalls that while living in Little Water Hen, she had not written a single line that gave her satisfaction. She speaks of being aware that she was absorbing and storing people, sights and sounds of a life she would write about. There in her recollection of her own journey to Water Hen country, we meet the character who would later become Isaac Boussorvski. The names Côté and O'Rorke appear. The kindly station master who takes pity on the young author during her long wait for the train to Rorketon would appear in Luzina's philosophy as she travels to Sainte Rose du Lac on her annual holiday: "Luzina had only to put herself under a human being's protection for him to behave toward her exactly as she wished."

Ten years after her stay in northern Manitoba, while in a foreign country, Roy gains "access" to her memories of the uncivilized wilderness of the Water Hen. In her essay, "My Manitoba Heritage," she observes, "The most enduring thing Manitoba gave me was the memory of its landscape." In the novel, the sometimes pastoral, often harsh landscape of this region serves to encapsulate and isolate a world composed of many diverse nationalities who "could get along so well together, gossip, laugh, and sing together," irrefutable proof, the world-travelled and multilingual Capuchin observes, "that mankind is made for peace!"

Luzina is round and soft, her face shines with inner contentment, and I imagine that she radiates the smell of raw pastry covering a saskatoon pie. She and Hippolyte are descendents of the risk-taking adventurers, the *coureurs de bois* and *coureurs de plaine* who came west and settled along the Red River in Saint Jean Baptiste and Letellier, small towns along the American border. As Luzina listens to Mademoiselle Côté relate the adventures of the French explorers in the New World, she comes to see herself and Hippolyte among these builders of the nation, and this thought makes her cry. She is brought back to reality by the demands of domesticity and the realization that her career in life is to serve others. She accepts this joyfully and finds recompense in everyday life, such as in her anticipation of her annual trip to Sainte Rose du Lac to give birth. She turns the journey into a grand adventure, an opportunity to satisfy her intense curiosity about the world around her, and she justifies this pleasure as "proper rewards for duty done."

While Luzina hungers for information, she is content to sit at the fringes of her family's education, catching only snippets while she darns a sock. The first day of lessons finds her bereft of her children. Now it is her turn to ask questions. Although piqued by their adoration of Mademoiselle Côté, Luzina is proud of their achievements and rejoices as the young teacher gives her children pride in the role France has played in the settlement of their country. When the rigid, prudish Miss O'Rorke replaces Mademoiselle Côté and attempts to subdue nature for the sake of her own comfort and to imprint her brand of civilization on their lives, Luzina, though puzzled by the woman's ways, accepts this awkward situation and chooses to see the benefit to her children of being confronted by another view of history and being given the opportunity to learn the English language. Then Armand Dubreuil arrives with his arsenal and blasts his way through summer. Hippolyte and Luzina, while appalled by the carnage, approach the man with tact and gentleness. Just as we are about to dislike the male teacher, he becomes "the best teacher of all."

Where Nests the Water Hen is peopled with eccentric characters: the postman, Nick Sluzick; the tight-fisted trader, Isaac Boussorvski; and the good-natured warm Capuchin, Father Joseph-Marie. The Capuchin, though well-educated and world-travelled, is as childlike as Luzina. His feelings of love for man and for God are strongest when he takes to the road to minister to the outlying parishes. Like Luzina, he is tolerant of other religions and nationalities. She is born to serve and he to love. Her desire to provide an education for her children mirrors his desire, as he obtains a bell, a harmonium, and a Presbyterian organist for his mission at Rorketon, for "the ultimate embellishment of perfection for his missions." The eccentricities of these characters are treated with humour and acceptance. In this isolated north country the people depend upon one another, and everyone's business *is*, of necessity, everyone's business. The landscape encourages unity regardless of people's race or creed.

The daily caring for a large family causes time to pass quickly, and, before she and we realize, Luzina's job is complete and the hands on the clock appear to stop moving. Winters are long. Luzina remains attached to her scattered children through letters, their envelopes addressed by the remaining "surprise" child so that Luzina's uneven script might not embarrass them. We would have Luzina a pathetic figure, sitting on a chair in the doorway with her plump idle hands folded in her lap, looking into the blaze of the setting sun on water and listening to the bleating of sheep and the sharp wild cries of the water hen. A rather sad, abandoned figure. But time climbs up the side of the egg, around the top of it to the beginning, and, instead, we leave Luzina in the presence of Father Joseph-Marie and Mademoiselle Côté in the arms of Hippolyte, and as they dance Luzina turns her young, round, and sensual face up to him and smiles.

I RECALL seeing a photograph of Gabrielle Roy and of reading about her achievements years ago when I was very young and lived in southern Manitoba. I was awed by the fact that a renowned author had grown up in St. Boniface. I spent weeks in the summer visiting cousins there on Rue Eugenie and often crossed the Norwood bridge with my grandmère to the "English" side of the river to shop at Eaton's. I listened to her mild complaints about clerks who could or would not speak French. It was rumoured that there were Roys in the high branches of my father's family tree, and I imagined that we were related and that the author and I resembled each other.

Many years would pass before I would read Gabrielle

Roy's work, and each time I came upon it, the time seemed exactly right. When I read *The Road Past Altamont*, for instance, I was living in a village in the Pembina Hills, cheek to cheek with the town of Altamont, and I often drove along the road past the town. I recognized myself as the child in "The Old Man and the Child," in her wonder as she views the great inland sea, Lake Winnipeg, for the first time. While living in Winnipeg among hard-working immigrants, the poor, the dispirited, I met Florentine from *The Tin Flute* and wept because I understood the "why" of this tenacious, gritty character, a vain, flirtatious spinner of dreams. I lived alongside the people who vanished during the night leaving behind the bitter stain of despair and understood Rose-Anna and her anxiety for her vulnerable brood. *Where Nests the Water Hen* came to me when I was living outside my province for the first time and when there was a need to return to the perceived uncomplicated landscape of childhood.

I believe that years ago I met a woman just like Luzina in a bus depot in Winnipeg. She had just arrived from a town in the west. Notre Dame de Loudres, I recall. She was short, round, soft-looking, with kinky light brown hair. Her broad face shone with perspiration and happiness as she related to me her mission. She was going to enter a convent and become the bride of Jesus. A handstitched bag at her feet bulged with all she possessed. Her stocky bare legs were pock-marked with the swellings of mosquito bites. What would she do as a bride of Jesus, I wondered. Anything, she said. Scrub floors, cook, anything. I searched for the quiver of fear in her rotund hen's bosom, the flicker of uncertainty in her eyes, or the fever of fanaticism. But there was none of these. Later, she wrote to me. She was happy. She was all that she was.

As I close the pages on the soft summer Manitoba night of *Where Nests the Water Hen*, its swarms of mosquitoes, the music and the dance, I have the feeling that I have returned from a time far removed from the novel's actual setting and that the landscape and the story have been viewed by both the author and her reader through that opaque veil of time, through eyes misted with longing for a return to innocence.

BY GABRIELLE ROY

AUTOBIOGRAPHY
La Détresse et l'enchantement [*Enchantment and Sorrow*]
(1984)

ESSAYS AND MEMORIES
Cet été qui chantait [*Enchanted Summer*] (1972)
Fragiles Lumières de la terre
[*The Fragile Lights of Earth*] (1978)
De quoi t'ennuies-tu, Eveline?
[*What Are You Lonely For, Eveline?*] (1982)

FICTION
Bonheur d'occasion [*The Tin Flute*] (1945)
La Petite Poule d'Eau [*Where Nests the Water Hen*]
(1950)
Alexandre Chenevert [*The Cashier*] (1954)
Rue Deschambault [*Street of Riches*] (1955)
La Montagne secrète [*The Hidden Mountain*] (1961)
La Route d'Altamont [*The Road Past Altamont*] (1966)
La Rivière sans repos [*Windflower*] (1970)
Un jardin au bout du monde [*Garden in the Wind*] (1975)
Ces enfants de ma vie [*Children of My Heart*] (1977)